Eli and the Wish Trees

Diversity, Equality, and Inclusion

Finn Hayes

Published by Whimsy Tales Press, 2024.

This is a work of fiction. Similarities to real people, places, or events are entirely coincidental.

ELI AND THE WISH TREES

First edition. November 19, 2024.

Copyright © 2024 Finn Hayes.

ISBN: 979-8230188308

Written by Finn Hayes.

Table of Contents

Dedication 1
Preface 2
Chapter 1: The Discovery of the Wish Trees 3
Chapter 2: Meeting the Trees 7
Chapter 3: The Tree of Generosity 11
Chapter 4: The Tree of Patience 15
Chapter 5: The Tree of Gratitude 18
Chapter 6: Learning about the Tree of Courage 22
Chapter 7: The Tree of Honesty 26
Chapter 8: A Lesson from the Tree of Humility 30
Chapter 9: Discovering the Tree of Friendship 34
Chapter 10: The Tree of Respect 38
Chapter 11: The Tree of Kindness in Action 42
Chapter 12: The Tree of Forgiveness 46
Chapter 13: Celebrating the Tree of Unity 50
Chapter 14: The Tree of Hope 54
Chapter 15: Learning from the Tree of Gratitude in Action 58
Chapter 16: The Tree of Acceptance 62
Chapter 17: The Tree of Resilience 66
Chapter 18: The Tree of Empathy 69
Chapter 19: The Tree of Patience 73
Chapter 20: The Tree of Generosity 77
Chapter 21: The Tree of Humility 81
Chapter 22: The Tree of Courage 85
Chapter 23: The Tree of Wisdom 88
Chapter 24: The Tree of Joy 91
Chapter 25: The Tree of Unity 94

Dedication

To all the young hearts with dreams of a kinder world, this book is for you. May you find the courage to be compassionate, the strength to stand together, and the joy in embracing all the beauty that makes each of us unique. I dedicate this story to the wisdom of children who see the world with open hearts, and to the teachers—whether parents, friends, or nature itself—who nurture the seeds of kindness, unity, and understanding within each one of us. May these lessons grow with you and blossom into a world full of love and light.

Preface

The world is a beautiful, diverse tapestry woven together by countless stories, and through this book, I hope to introduce young readers to the power of unity, empathy, and kindness. *Eli and the Wish Trees* is not just a story about learning important values; it is a journey that teaches children to embrace differences, recognize their inner strengths, and connect with the world around them. Each tree in Eli's journey represents a unique lesson, showing him—and readers—that every person, creature, and moment has something valuable to offer. Through Eli's interactions with the Wish Trees, children will discover the beauty of living with compassion and courage, and find inspiration to bring kindness and understanding into their daily lives. I hope this story becomes a cherished companion that guides young readers on a journey of self-discovery and connection, nurturing the seeds of love, joy, and unity within them.

Chapter 1: The Discovery of the Wish Trees

Eli's summer mornings usually began like any other kid's. He'd wake up early, ready to explore the small but familiar corners of his world: the backyard, his favorite path to the park, and the sprawling green spaces that lay beyond the old oak trees. Eli loved exploring because he never knew what he might find; every leaf, rock, and feather he picked up had its own secret. Today, however, he would stumble upon something extraordinary that would change his life forever.

It was a warm morning, and Eli was feeling particularly adventurous. He had just finished breakfast and, slinging a small backpack over his shoulder, hurried outside, eager to see what surprises the day had in store. The park was already buzzing with life as he approached it. Birds chirped cheerfully in the trees, squirrels darted up and down the trunks, and a gentle breeze whispered through the branches. The air was thick with the scent of freshly cut grass and wildflowers. As he passed by the flower beds, he noticed how the bees were busy at work, buzzing from one vibrant blossom to the next. Eli loved the park and its peaceful magic.

But something was different today. As Eli crossed the park's stone path, his attention was caught by a glimmering light near the grove. It was faint, like a soft golden sparkle just barely visible in the morning sunlight. Curious, Eli walked off the path and into the grove, brushing aside branches as he went deeper into the trees. The air seemed cooler here, the light more filtered. Each step brought him closer to the mysterious shimmer.

As he neared, he found himself in a clearing he had never noticed before. It was tucked away, almost hidden within the park, but its presence was unmistakable. A circle of tall, ancient trees with branches that twisted and curled in intricate patterns surrounded the clearing.

Eli marveled at the trees. They were unlike anything he had seen; each tree was unique, with bark of different textures and colors, leaves in every imaginable shape, and branches that seemed to reach out to each other as if they were holding hands in a leafy dance.

At the center of this ring of trees, a gentle glow pulsed, casting a warm, inviting light. Eli felt a strange mixture of excitement and calmness wash over him as he approached. It was as if these trees had been waiting for him. He reached out a hand and touched the bark of the nearest tree. It felt surprisingly warm, almost alive. And then, he heard it—a soft voice, like a gentle breeze, speaking to him from within the tree.

"Welcome, Eli," the voice said warmly, filling him with a sense of comfort. Eli stepped back, wide-eyed. He glanced around to see if anyone else was there, but it was just him and the trees.

"Who... who are you?" Eli whispered, half expecting that he might be imagining things.

"We are the Wish Trees," the voice continued, coming from all around him. "We've been here for a long time, watching over this park, sharing kindness with those who seek it. And today, we've chosen to reveal ourselves to you."

Eli's heart raced with excitement. Wish Trees? He had never heard of such a thing! The voice continued, as if reading his mind. "Each one of us holds a special gift, a power that only kindness and good intentions can unlock. We grant wishes, Eli. But our wishes are not for ordinary things; they're for those who wish with kindness in their hearts."

Eli couldn't believe what he was hearing. Trees that granted wishes? It was the kind of magic he had only read about in storybooks. He looked at each tree, noticing how they seemed to have their own personalities. Some trees were tall and majestic, with thick, strong branches, while others were slender and graceful, their branches drooping like willows. Every tree was unique, like a person with their own story to tell.

The tree with the golden leaves seemed to sense his wonder and spoke to him directly. "Would you like to make a wish, Eli?"

Eli thought for a moment, his mind racing with possibilities. He could wish for a new bike or the ability to fly, but something held him back. Somehow, he felt that this was not about material things or superpowers. These trees were asking for something deeper, something that came from the heart. So, he closed his eyes and thought carefully about what he truly wanted.

Finally, he whispered, "I wish... to make a new friend."

The golden-leaved tree glowed warmly, and a gentle breeze swirled around him, making the leaves rustle softly. The tree's voice came again, calm and kind. "Your wish is pure, Eli. Friendship is a gift that grows like us, with time and care. Walk with kindness, and your wish will come true."

Eli felt a rush of warmth inside. It was as if he had been given a secret he would carry forever. As he opened his eyes, he saw a faint sparkle around him, like stardust drifting in the air. He knew something magical had happened, even if he couldn't quite explain it.

That day, as he left the grove, Eli felt different. He felt a little braver, a little kinder. The world around him seemed brighter, too, as if he could see all the little details he had missed before. The leaves on the trees sparkled in the sun, and the flowers seemed to bloom just for him. He made his way through the park, still feeling the magic of the Wish Trees within him.

As he passed the playground, he noticed a boy sitting alone on one of the swings. The boy looked about Eli's age, with sandy hair and a curious expression on his face. Remembering his wish, Eli felt a nudge of courage. Maybe this was the friend he had wished for.

"Hi, I'm Eli," he said, approaching the boy with a friendly smile. "Do you want to play?"

The boy looked up, surprised, but his face quickly broke into a grin. "I'm Max. Sure! I was just waiting for someone to play with."

Eli felt his heart lift as they ran to the slides, laughing and talking as if they had known each other forever. He couldn't believe how easy it was to make a friend. Max told him about his favorite games, and Eli shared stories about his explorations in the park. They played until the sun began to dip in the sky, painting the horizon with shades of orange and pink.

As they walked back home, Eli thought about the Wish Trees and the magical promise they held. He knew he'd be visiting them again, and he was excited to share what he had learned with others. With each step, he felt like he was carrying a secret treasure—a gift that could spread to everyone he met.

Eli looked up at the sky, the stars beginning to twinkle. He knew he wasn't just carrying a wish; he was carrying a piece of the magic that the Wish Trees had shared with him. It wasn't just about getting what he wanted. It was about understanding the joy that kindness and friendship could

Chapter 2: Meeting the Trees

The next morning, Eli was up before the first rays of sunlight peeked over the rooftops. He was too excited to sleep in, his mind still buzzing from the previous day's discovery. He kept replaying the moment he had touched the golden-leaved tree, felt its warmth, and heard its soft voice. He knew there was more to learn, and he couldn't wait to return to the park to explore the Wish Trees again.

With a quiet tiptoe through the house, he quickly got dressed, grabbed his backpack, and slipped out the door. The streets were peaceful, and the world felt like it was still waking up, but Eli's heart was wide awake and ready for adventure. By the time he reached the park, the sun had just begun to rise, casting a soft golden glow over the trees and flowers. The park felt familiar, but today it held a special kind of magic.

He made his way past the playground, across the meadow, and into the grove where he had met the Wish Trees. As he stepped into the hidden clearing, a sense of warmth and belonging washed over him. It was as if the trees had been waiting for him, welcoming him back like an old friend. The trees stood silent, their leaves rustling softly in the breeze, but Eli sensed that they were aware of his presence. He approached the golden-leaved tree, the same one he had touched yesterday, and placed his hand on its bark once more.

"Welcome back, Eli," the tree's gentle voice echoed in his mind, sounding like a whisper carried by the wind. Eli felt a rush of excitement and awe. He wanted to know more about these magical beings and the world of wishes they held within their branches.

"Thank you," Eli replied, a bit shyly. "I... I'm so happy to be here. I still can't believe you're real."

"Oh, we are very real," the tree replied with a warm chuckle. "And each of us has a story, just as every leaf and branch has a purpose. Today, if you'd like, we can introduce you to some of our friends."

Eli nodded eagerly, his eyes wide with anticipation. He noticed that the trees surrounding him seemed to shimmer in the morning sunlight, as if each one were glowing with its own unique light. Slowly, the other trees began to "speak" as well. It wasn't a sound in the usual sense but a feeling, like thoughts carried on a gentle breeze that reached him even without words.

The first tree to speak had dark, sturdy bark and thick branches covered with broad, emerald-green leaves. It radiated a sense of calm strength, like an old friend who always knew the right thing to say. Eli felt a sense of wisdom coming from this tree, as though it had witnessed many years and held countless secrets within its core.

"Hello, Eli," the tree said, its voice slow and deep, filling Eli with a feeling of comfort and patience. "I am Sage. I have watched over this grove for many, many years, and I have seen kindness blossom in ways both big and small. My gift is to help those who seek understanding and patience. I can see that you have a heart open to learning, and I am glad to meet you."

Eli was captivated by Sage's voice, which seemed to hold both the weight of ancient stories and the gentle compassion of a loving guardian. He realized that Sage was not only wise but also deeply kind. Somehow, he felt that Sage understood him in a way that went beyond words.

Just as Eli was about to respond, he felt a new presence beside him. This tree had soft, silvery bark that shimmered like moonlight and delicate leaves that swayed gracefully even in the gentlest breeze. Its voice was light and musical, filling the air with a sense of peace and hope.

"Welcome, Eli," it said, its tone bright and airy. "I am Willow, the bringer of dreams and hopes. My branches reach far and wide, gathering wishes from those who seek joy and understanding. If you are ever feeling lost or in need of comfort, know that I am here to help you find your way."

ELI AND THE WISH TREES

Eli felt a wave of peace wash over him as he listened to Willow's words. Her voice was like a lullaby, soothing and comforting. He reached out to touch her trunk, feeling a softness that seemed to radiate kindness and warmth. He closed his eyes, imagining all the hopes and dreams that Willow must have gathered over the years. He thought of his own wish from the previous day, the one for friendship, and felt a surge of gratitude. Perhaps Willow had played a part in helping him meet Max.

After a moment, Eli opened his eyes and looked around, noticing yet another tree with bark that was rough and craggy, like the surface of a mountain. This tree stood tall and proud, with sturdy branches reaching up to the sky. Its leaves were a deep, dark green, and it exuded an air of resilience and courage. Eli felt a thrill of excitement as he sensed the tree's powerful presence.

"I am Oak," the tree declared, its voice strong and steady. "I am the keeper of courage and strength. Those who face challenges with bravery find their wishes granted through me. Remember, Eli, courage is not the absence of fear but the ability to stand tall in spite of it."

Eli felt a shiver of awe as he listened to Oak's words. He realized that courage wasn't just about being brave in the face of danger; it was about standing by his friends, even when things were tough. Oak's strength and conviction filled him with a newfound sense of purpose, and he felt braver just by being in the tree's presence.

As he stood there, absorbing everything Oak had shared, Eli noticed a gentle rustling behind him. Turning, he saw a smaller tree with smooth, light-colored bark and tiny, delicate leaves that quivered like little hearts in the breeze. The tree's presence was gentle and comforting, and its voice was soft and reassuring.

"Hello, Eli," it whispered, its voice like the soft rustle of leaves on a quiet day. "I am Birch, the tree of kindness and compassion. I grant wishes to those who show care for others, those who see the world through gentle eyes and open hearts. In kindness, you find the seeds of true friendship."

Eli's heart filled with warmth as he listened to Birch's words. He thought about the kindness he felt from his new friend Max and how much it had meant to him. He knew that showing kindness was more than just being polite; it was about opening his heart to others, just as Birch had said.

Chapter 3: The Tree of Generosity

Eli could hardly contain his excitement as he returned to the park. Each day spent with the Wish Trees revealed new mysteries, filling him with a deeper sense of purpose and connection. He walked briskly toward the hidden grove, eager to learn from the trees and maybe even make another wish. Today, he had brought his friend Lila with him. Lila was curious about the grove Eli had described, and she listened wide-eyed as he told her about the magic of the Wish Trees. Lila had a gentle, compassionate heart, and Eli felt she was the perfect person to share his secret with.

As they stepped into the grove, the Wish Trees greeted them with a rustling of leaves, as if they were whispering their welcome. Lila's face lit up with wonder. She had seen trees her whole life but had never felt anything quite like this. The trees here seemed almost alive, their branches bending slightly as if acknowledging her presence. She looked at Eli with a mix of excitement and disbelief.

"Are they really magical?" Lila asked, her voice barely above a whisper.

"Yes," Eli replied, his voice full of reverence. "Each one of them has a unique power, and they grant wishes if you ask with kindness."

Just as Eli finished speaking, a nearby tree with thick branches and deep, lush green leaves seemed to shimmer. Its trunk was broad and sturdy, with bark that was slightly twisted, giving it an ancient and wise appearance. The tree's branches hung low, almost as if inviting them closer. Eli could feel a warm, comforting energy coming from the tree. He reached out his hand, and Lila did the same, both of them placing their palms on the rough bark.

A gentle voice spoke in their minds, soft yet filled with a warm strength. "Welcome, Eli and Lila. I am Elm, the Tree of Generosity. I bring gifts to those who understand the value of giving freely, without expecting anything in return. Generosity is a gift you give with your heart, and it can make the world a brighter place."

Eli felt a shiver of excitement. Generosity! It was a word he had heard many times, but he realized that he had never truly thought about what it meant. Giving something away without expecting anything back? It sounded simple, but somehow he felt that there was more to it. Lila's eyes sparkled with curiosity as she leaned closer, eager to learn from Elm's wisdom.

"Generosity is about sharing what you have," Elm continued. "It can be as simple as sharing a smile, a kind word, or a small treasure with someone who needs it. True generosity fills the giver's heart with joy, even more than it helps the one who receives."

The tree's words were like a melody in Eli's mind, filling him with a sense of peace and purpose. He thought about the things he valued—his toys, his snacks, even his time. Could he share those with others without expecting anything back? He glanced at Lila, who seemed deep in thought as well.

Then, as if on cue, Elm's branches began to shimmer and sway, creating a tiny golden light that floated down toward Eli and Lila. They watched in awe as the light took shape, forming a small, radiant leaf that glowed with a warm, amber light. Elm's gentle voice continued, "Take this leaf as a reminder. When you share, let your heart be as open and generous as the branches of a tree. Only then will you experience the true joy that generosity brings."

Eli reached out and caught the glowing leaf, feeling its warmth in his hands. He knew that it wasn't an ordinary leaf—it was a symbol of the lesson Elm had shared with them. He carefully placed it in his backpack, promising himself to remember Elm's words.

"Thank you, Elm," he said, bowing slightly to show his respect. Lila nodded as well, her eyes full of gratitude.

Eli and Lila spent the rest of the afternoon exploring the grove and talking about what they had learned. As they wandered, they began to notice small opportunities for generosity around them. Lila pointed out a squirrel struggling to find food, and without hesitation, Eli pulled a few crumbs from his pocket and scattered them on the ground. The squirrel eagerly gathered the crumbs, and Eli felt a warmth inside that was hard to describe. It was a simple gesture, but it made him feel connected to the world around him in a new way.

As they continued walking, they saw a group of younger kids playing nearby. One of the children was struggling to climb up a small hill. Lila and Eli exchanged a glance and, without needing to say a word, walked over to offer their help. They took the child's hands and, with a little teamwork, helped him reach the top. The child's face broke into a wide grin, and Eli and Lila felt that same warmth again.

By the time the sun began to set, Eli and Lila were filled with a sense of quiet happiness. They realized that generosity wasn't just about giving things away; it was about noticing when someone needed a bit of help or kindness and being willing to offer it. They had started with small acts, but each one made them feel a little lighter and a little more connected to the world.

As they left the park, Lila turned to Eli and said, "Do you think Elm knows about every act of generosity we do?"

Eli thought for a moment. "Maybe. Or maybe it's more about how we feel when we give. Elm taught us that generosity should come from the heart. So, even if no one else sees, I think it still matters."

They both fell into a thoughtful silence, each reflecting on the day's experiences. Eli felt a sense of accomplishment, knowing that he had made a difference, however small. He realized that generosity wasn't something that had to be grand or flashy; it could be quiet and gentle, like a tree giving shade on a hot day.

As they parted ways, Eli couldn't wait to return to the grove. The Wish Trees had taught him another beautiful lesson, and he knew there was much more to learn. Elm's words echoed in his mind as he walked home, a melody of kindness and giving that stayed with him long after the sun had disappeared from the sky.

Chapter 4: The Tree of Patience

The following week was filled with excitement for Eli. Each day after school, he felt the pull of the Wish Trees, an irresistible urge to visit the grove and learn more about the magic hidden within each tree. So, when Saturday finally arrived, Eli grabbed his backpack, tossed in a few snacks, and headed to the park without delay. This time, he walked slower than usual, noticing the way the world around him seemed to breathe and flow with its own rhythm. The leaves on the trees swayed softly in the breeze, and the park's quiet energy reminded him that there was more to learn if he just took his time.

When Eli arrived at the grove, he took a deep breath, feeling the familiar warmth of the Wish Trees surrounding him. Each tree seemed to emit its own energy, and today, one particular tree caught his attention. This tree was different from the others. It had dark, rugged bark with long, winding branches that twisted and curled as if they had grown slowly over centuries. Its leaves were a soft, calming green, their edges lined with a faint silver hue that shimmered in the sunlight. Eli felt a sense of tranquility radiating from the tree, a quiet strength that seemed to invite him closer.

Eli approached the tree, placing his hand on its rough bark. As he did, he felt a warmth spread from his fingers up through his arm and into his heart. The tree's voice entered his mind, slow and steady, each word carrying a sense of calm and wisdom.

"Welcome, Eli," the tree said in a voice as smooth as a gentle breeze. "I am Cypress, the Tree of Patience. Patience is a gift that grows within those who take the time to understand and appreciate the world around them. I teach the art of waiting, of finding peace in each moment rather than rushing ahead."

Eli listened carefully, intrigued by Cypress's words. Patience was something he had always struggled with, especially when it came to things he was excited about. He often found himself tapping his foot, glancing at the clock, or fidgeting while waiting for something to happen. But Cypress spoke about patience as if it were something beautiful, something that could be as rewarding as any gift or wish.

"What does it mean to be patient?" Eli asked, genuinely curious. "Is it just about waiting?"

Cypress's branches seemed to sway thoughtfully, as though considering Eli's question. "Patience is more than just waiting, Eli," the tree replied. "It is learning to embrace the moment, finding peace within yourself even when things do not happen as quickly as you would like. It is trusting that everything has its own time and place."

Eli pondered Cypress's words, feeling a quietness settle over him. The tree seemed to sense his thoughts and continued, "Think of the way I grow, Eli. Year by year, season by season, I reach toward the sky. I do not hurry, for I know that each moment is a part of my journey. Just as I grow slowly, with care and purpose, so too does patience grow within you."

As Cypress spoke, Eli noticed that each word seemed to sink deep into his heart, calming the little restlessness that often bubbled within him. He imagined what it would be like to grow slowly, to embrace each step of his journey rather than rushing toward the next thing. Cypress's voice was like a lullaby, soothing and steady, and Eli felt himself relax more with every word.

The tree then suggested something that surprised him. "Today, Eli, I would like you to practice patience. Find a quiet spot, sit down, and simply observe. Notice the world around you without expecting anything to happen. Feel the breeze, listen to the birds, and let time unfold naturally."

Eli nodded, willing to give it a try. He wandered a few steps away from Cypress, found a comfortable spot under a smaller tree nearby, and sat down. At first, he fidgeted, feeling a familiar urge to look around for something exciting. But remembering Cypress's words, he took a deep breath and focused on the sounds around him. He listened to the wind rustling through the leaves, the soft chirping of birds nearby, and the distant laughter of children playing in the park. He noticed the subtle shift in light as the clouds drifted lazily across the sky, casting shadows that danced on the ground.

As the minutes passed, Eli found himself relaxing even more. He began to notice the small details he usually overlooked—the way ants marched in a line, carrying tiny bits of leaves back to their nest, the way a butterfly flitted from flower to flower, its wings painted in colors that seemed almost too beautiful to be real. Each moment felt full and vibrant, as if he were seeing the world for the first time.

For a long while, Eli sat in silence, feeling a peacefulness he hadn't known before. It was a quiet joy, one that didn't require action or excitement, just a simple appreciation of being present. The concept of time seemed to drift away, and all that mattered was the here and now.

Finally, he stood up, feeling a calm energy flowing through him. He walked back to Cypress, a smile spreading across his face. "I think I understand now," he said. "Patience isn't just about waiting—it's about being part of each moment and finding peace within it."

Cypress's branches swayed in approval, and Eli felt the tree's warm presence filling his heart once more. "You have learned well, Eli. Remember, patience is not always easy, but it will help you see the world with clearer eyes and appreciate each step of your journey. You will find that patience can bring you closer to others, as it helps you understand their needs and rhythms."

Chapter 5: The Tree of Gratitude

On a crisp, clear morning, Eli awoke with a sense of wonder still lingering from his recent lessons with the Wish Trees. As he lay in bed, the memories of kindness, patience, and generosity filled him with a warmth that made the world seem just a little brighter. Today, he felt an urge to visit the grove once again, hoping to find out what new wisdom awaited him. Without hesitation, he dressed quickly, grabbed his backpack, and headed to the park.

The air was fresh, carrying the earthy scent of leaves and soil, as though the whole park had been freshly painted in greens and browns by the early morning dew. When Eli reached the grove, he took a deep breath, letting the calming energy of the Wish Trees fill him. This place had become more than just a hidden spot in the park; it was a sanctuary, a world where each tree held a special piece of wisdom, patiently waiting for someone to discover it.

Today, a tree with soft, golden-brown bark and delicate branches caught Eli's attention. It wasn't the largest or the tallest tree in the grove, but something about its presence felt welcoming and humble. The leaves were a mix of green and amber, with hints of deep red, like autumn captured in a single frame. Eli felt a pull toward it, as if this tree had a story it wanted to share with him.

He approached, placing his hand on the warm, slightly textured bark. Almost immediately, a soothing voice filled his mind, gentle yet filled with a joy that made him feel lighter, as though he were standing in a beam of sunlight.

"Welcome, Eli," the tree said, its voice like the melody of a song. "I am Maple, the Tree of Gratitude. My gift is to remind those who visit me of the blessings that surround them. Gratitude is the key to seeing beauty in every corner of life, even in the simplest of things."

Eli felt a twinge of surprise. Gratitude was a word he had heard many times, but it was often tied to saying "thank you" for gifts or favors. Maple seemed to be talking about something deeper—a kind of gratitude that went beyond polite manners. He listened closely, sensing that this lesson would help him see the world in a way he hadn't before.

"Gratitude is a light that shines within you," Maple continued. "It's a way of noticing the gifts around you, from the warmth of the sun to the comfort of a friend's smile. It allows us to appreciate both the grand and the small, finding joy even in the challenges we face."

Eli nodded slowly, absorbing Maple's words. Gratitude as a light—it was a beautiful thought. He wondered how he could practice this kind of gratitude, how he could feel thankful for everything around him. Maple seemed to sense his question and spoke again.

"To practice gratitude, start with small things," the tree said. "Close your eyes and think of three things that brought you joy today. Let your heart fill with appreciation for these moments, no matter how small they may seem."

Eli closed his eyes, focusing on the first three things that came to mind. He thought about the warmth of his bed when he first woke up, the cheerful chirping of birds outside his window, and the comforting feeling of the park as he walked through it. Each thought brought a smile to his face, and he felt a sense of warmth spread through him, like a soft glow that made everything seem just a little bit better.

When he opened his eyes, Maple's branches shimmered softly, as though approving of Eli's effort. Eli felt a gentle joy blooming within him, a joy that didn't come from anything new or exciting, but from appreciating what was already there.

"Gratitude is like a treasure chest," Maple continued, "filled with moments of joy that we often overlook. When you focus on what you have, rather than what you lack, you open that treasure chest and allow its light to shine. This light helps you through hard times and brings peace to your heart."

Eli thought about Maple's words and nodded thoughtfully. He realized that he often spent time wishing for things he didn't have or focusing on what he wanted next. But here, standing with Maple, he felt that his life was already filled with treasures he had been too busy to notice.

Just then, Maple's branches stirred, and Eli felt a soft breeze brush against his face, carrying the faintest scent of sweet maple syrup. Maple's voice spoke again, softer this time, as though sharing a secret.

"Gratitude is also about sharing," Maple said. "When you express thankfulness, you spread joy to others, just as I share my shade, my leaves, and my branches with those who visit me. Gratitude grows when it is shared, like a ripple in a pond that spreads far and wide."

Eli thought about how he could share his gratitude. He remembered his parents, who worked hard to take care of him and make sure he had everything he needed. He thought of his friends, like Lila and Max, who shared their laughter, kindness, and time with him. Even the teachers at school, who sometimes gave him extra help when he struggled with a subject. He felt a surge of appreciation for each of them, realizing that they were all part of his life's treasures.

Before he knew it, Eli was filled with an idea. He decided to make a small gratitude journal, where he could write down all the things he was thankful for each day. And perhaps, he could even share this with others, encouraging them to do the same.

Maple's leaves rustled in encouragement as if approving of his plan. Eli felt a sense of calm satisfaction, knowing that he had found a way to keep Maple's lesson close to his heart. He reached up and placed his hand on the tree once more, feeling its warmth and quiet strength.

"Thank you, Maple," he said softly. "I'll carry this lesson with me, and I'll try to see the treasures around me every day."

Maple's branches dipped in response, almost like a gentle bow, and a single golden leaf drifted down, landing softly in Eli's hand. He held the leaf carefully, knowing it was a symbol of the lesson he had learned—a reminder to live with gratitude, to see the beauty in each day, and to share that joy with others.

As he left the grove, Eli felt a new energy within him, one that made the colors of the world seem a little brighter and the sounds a little clearer. He walked through the park with a smile on his face, feeling thankful for every step he took, every tree he passed, and every breath of fresh air.

On his way home, he noticed a small group of children playing nearby. One of them tripped and fell, letting out a small cry. Eli's heart filled with empathy, and he walked over, offering a hand to help the child up. He gave the child a reassuring smile, feeling grateful that he could bring a bit of comfort to someone else.

When he finally reached home, Eli sat down at his desk and pulled out a small notebook. On the first page, he wrote in neat letters: "My Gratitude Journal." Underneath, he began to list all the things he had felt thankful for that day. By the time he finished, his heart felt full, and he knew that Maple's lesson would stay with him forever.

As he closed the journal, he noticed the golden leaf resting nearby. He gently tucked it between the pages, knowing it would be there whenever he needed a reminder to look for the light in his life. He didn't need grand adventures or special gifts to feel happy; he had everything he needed within his own heart.

Chapter 6: Learning about the Tree of Courage

Eli woke up early, filled with a mixture of excitement and nervousness. Today, he planned to visit the Wish Trees again. Although his heart was eager to learn, he couldn't help but feel a little hesitant. Courage wasn't something he thought much about until now, but lately, he had been feeling the stirrings of bravery, a subtle urge to face challenges he had once shied away from.

As he walked through the park toward the grove, Eli reflected on what courage might mean. He'd always thought of courage as something only heroes in stories had, something reserved for knights or adventurers, but recently he had started to wonder if it was something ordinary people needed, too. Could he find bravery in small acts? Could he discover strength within himself?

When he entered the grove, the familiar warmth of the Wish Trees greeted him, putting him at ease. Each tree felt like a friend now, each with its own personality and wisdom. Eli took a moment to breathe in the peaceful energy of the grove before he noticed one tree standing a little apart from the others. This tree was strong and tall, its bark thick and gnarled, as if it had weathered countless storms. Its branches stretched high into the sky, and its leaves were a deep, steadfast green that seemed to hold a quiet power. Eli felt a magnetic pull toward the tree, sensing that it had a lesson waiting for him.

Eli approached, reaching out to touch the rough bark. The tree's surface felt solid, grounding, and as he closed his eyes, he heard a voice, deep and steady, like the rumble of distant thunder.

"Hello, Eli," the tree greeted him, its voice warm but commanding. "I am Oak, the Tree of Courage. I am here to help you find the strength within yourself. Courage is not about having no fear; it is about choosing to act even when fear is present."

Eli felt his heartbeat quicken. Courage had always seemed like something difficult, even impossible. He remembered times when he had wanted to try something new but had held back because of fear—fear of failing, fear of being laughed at, fear of making mistakes. But Oak's words seemed to open a new understanding, as if courage wasn't about being fearless but about something deeper.

"What do you mean by choosing to act?" Eli asked, curiosity brightening his eyes.

Oak's branches swayed gently, as if gathering its thoughts before speaking. "Every day, we face moments that test our bravery. Some of these moments are small—like speaking up, trying something new, or standing up for a friend. Others may seem larger, requiring more strength than we think we have. But courage is always there, waiting for us to reach for it, to take that first step despite our fears. It's about trusting in your ability to handle what comes next, even if you're unsure."

Eli listened, feeling a calm strength flow from Oak. He thought about his own fears, the moments when he had felt uncertain. He thought about the time he had wanted to join the soccer team but had held back because he worried he wouldn't be good enough. He remembered his hesitation whenever he had to speak in front of his classmates, the way his heart would race and his voice would catch in his throat. Each time, he had felt as if he lacked the courage to move forward. But Oak's words were making him see courage in a new way, as a choice, a decision to act even when he was afraid.

Oak seemed to sense Eli's reflection and continued speaking. "Imagine, Eli, that every challenge is a mountain. Courage is the determination to begin the climb, to take one step at a time, trusting that you can reach the top. Sometimes, you may stumble; sometimes, you may need to rest. But each step you take, even when you feel afraid, is a victory of courage over fear."

Eli thought about this, imagining himself at the base of a tall mountain. The idea of climbing was intimidating, but something about Oak's words filled him with a quiet confidence. He could see himself taking that first step, then another, moving forward even if he didn't know exactly how he would reach the top.

"Is courage something that grows?" he asked, his voice filled with wonder.

"Yes, Eli," Oak replied gently. "Just as I have grown tall and strong over many years, so too does courage grow with each challenge you face. Every time you choose to face your fear, your courage becomes stronger, just like my roots digging deeper into the earth with each passing year. It is a part of you, as steady and resilient as my branches."

As Eli absorbed Oak's words, he felt a new determination forming within him. He realized that he wanted to practice courage, even if it meant facing his fears one small step at a time. Oak seemed to understand this, and its branches swayed in encouragement. The tree's energy wrapped around Eli like a protective shield, filling him with a strength he hadn't felt before.

Oak then spoke again, its voice steady and calm. "Would you like to try an act of courage today, Eli? A small step, one that will help you feel the strength within yourself?"

Eli hesitated but nodded, feeling a mixture of excitement and nervousness. He didn't know what Oak had in mind, but he trusted that it would be something he could manage. Oak's branches seemed to shimmer, and Eli felt a gentle nudge, a sense of support that made him feel braver.

"I want you to climb up one of my low branches," Oak said kindly. "It may seem simple, but climbing up into a tree requires trust—not only in yourself but also in the strength of the tree that holds you. Feel the courage within you and know that you are safe."

Eli looked at the sturdy branch Oak had pointed out. It wasn't very high, but it was still higher than he was used to climbing. He hesitated for a moment, feeling a flutter of fear in his stomach. But he remembered Oak's words about courage being a choice, about taking that first step. Gathering his resolve, he reached for the branch, gripping it firmly. Slowly, he placed one foot on the trunk, then the other, lifting himself up with care.

As he climbed, he felt his heartbeat quicken, but with each inch higher, his confidence grew. Soon, he was sitting on the branch, looking out over the grove. The view from above was beautiful; he could see the tops of the other Wish Trees swaying gently, the sunlight filtering through their leaves. A sense of accomplishment filled him. He had done it. It was a small climb, but to him, it felt like a great victory.

Oak's voice filled his mind once more, this time with a hint of pride. "Well done, Eli. This is how courage begins—with small steps that lead to greater heights. Remember this feeling. Each time you face your fears, no matter how small, you are strengthening the courage within you."

Eli nodded, feeling a surge of happiness. He climbed back down, a wide smile on his face, his heart filled with a newfound sense of bravery. The fear was still there, but now he knew he had the courage to face it. He realized that courage didn't mean his fears would disappear; it meant he could choose to move forward despite them.

Oak continued, "Courage also allows you to stand up for others, to speak up when you see something wrong, to offer kindness when others are afraid. It is not only for yourself but for those around you."

Eli thought about this, understanding that courage wasn't just for his own challenges. It was something he could use to help others, to stand by his friends, and to offer support to those who might need it. Oak had shown him that courage was a gift not only to himself but to the world.

Chapter 7: The Tree of Honesty

Eli had spent the last few days reflecting on all that the Wish Trees had taught him. His heart was full of gratitude, patience, generosity, and courage. Each lesson felt like a small treasure tucked into his pocket, ready to be drawn upon whenever he needed it. The park had become more than just a place to play; it was a world of wonder where each tree held a special wisdom.

Today, he felt a new kind of curiosity. He didn't know what the next lesson would be, but he sensed that he was ready for it. The morning sunlight filtered through his bedroom window as he got ready, filling him with a warmth that made him feel hopeful and excited. With a quick breakfast and a goodbye to his family, he set off to the park, eager to return to the grove and uncover what else the Wish Trees had to share.

As he entered the grove, he noticed a tree standing tall and straight, its trunk covered in smooth, pale bark that seemed to glow faintly in the morning light. The tree's branches were strong and orderly, stretching upward in a manner that gave it a noble appearance. Its leaves were bright green, almost shimmering as if reflecting the clear honesty of the sky above. Eli felt drawn to this tree, sensing that it held a powerful truth within it.

He approached and placed his hand on the cool, smooth bark. Almost instantly, he felt a calm strength flow through him, as if the tree was preparing him for a lesson that required courage and openness. A gentle, steady voice filled his mind, clear and direct.

"Hello, Eli," the tree greeted him in a tone that was both warm and firm. "I am Aspen, the Tree of Honesty. I guide those who seek to understand the power of truth. Honesty is the light that helps us see things clearly. It can be difficult to face sometimes, but it strengthens our hearts and builds trust with others."

Eli listened intently, realizing that this was indeed an important lesson. Honesty was something he understood on a surface level, like telling the truth when asked a question, but he sensed that Aspen was talking about something deeper—a truth that went beyond words.

Aspen continued, "Honesty is not just about avoiding lies, Eli. It's about being truthful with yourself and others, even when it's hard. It's about looking within, understanding your feelings, and being brave enough to share them with others. Honesty helps us to be real, to be seen as we truly are."

Eli thought about this, feeling both intrigued and a little nervous. Being honest with others was one thing, but being honest with himself—about his fears, his feelings, and his struggles—sounded challenging. He knew there were times he had hidden his true feelings, even from himself. There were times when he had pretended to be okay even when he felt hurt or scared, times when he had agreed with friends just to avoid disagreements.

Aspen's voice was gentle as it continued. "Honesty builds trust, Eli. When we are honest, we allow others to know us fully, and we strengthen our bonds with them. But honesty requires courage, for it often means being vulnerable, sharing parts of ourselves that we might otherwise want to keep hidden."

Eli nodded, thinking back to times when he had chosen to hide how he felt. He remembered once, when his friend Lila had accidentally broken a small toy he loved. She had apologized, but instead of telling her that he felt sad about it, he had brushed it off and pretended it didn't matter. Later, he felt frustrated, not with her, but with himself, for not sharing how he truly felt. Aspen's words made him realize that if he had been honest in that moment, it might have brought him and Lila closer, instead of creating a small, invisible wall between them.

Aspen seemed to sense Eli's reflections and continued, "Honesty helps us release burdens, Eli. When we hide parts of ourselves, we carry them alone. But when we are honest, we share that weight, allowing others to support us, to see us as we truly are. It frees our hearts and brings us peace."

Eli took a deep breath, feeling a mix of emotions. Aspen's lesson was teaching him something profound—that honesty wasn't just about speaking the truth but about living in truth, showing up as his real self, even when it was uncomfortable. He felt a desire to be more open, to let others see him, even the parts of him that felt messy or uncertain.

Aspen then suggested a small exercise. "Think of something you've held back from sharing, something that has been weighing on your heart. Today, I encourage you to find the courage to share this truth with someone close to you. It might feel vulnerable, but trust that honesty will bring a strength and closeness you may not yet see."

Eli thought about Aspen's suggestion and instantly knew what he wanted to do. He would talk to Lila about the time she had broken his toy. It was a small moment, but he felt it would be a way to practice honesty and let go of the small frustration he had held onto. He wasn't angry with Lila, but he felt that sharing his feelings would help him feel lighter and closer to her.

Thanking Aspen for the lesson, Eli left the grove and made his way to Lila's house. His heart pounded as he knocked on her door, his mind racing with thoughts of how he would explain his feelings. Lila answered the door with her usual bright smile, inviting him inside. They sat together in her living room, and after a moment of silence, Eli took a deep breath, deciding to share his truth.

"Lila," he began, his voice a little shaky, "I wanted to talk to you about something that's been on my mind. Do you remember when you accidentally broke my toy last month?"

Lila's smile faded, and she nodded, looking a bit guilty. "Yeah, I remember. I'm really sorry about that, Eli. I didn't mean to break it."

Eli smiled, appreciating her sincerity. "I know you didn't mean to, and I forgave you right away. But I didn't tell you the whole truth. I was actually a little sad when it happened because that toy was special to me. I acted like it didn't matter, but it really did."

Lila looked at him with understanding in her eyes. "I'm really sorry, Eli. I didn't know it meant so much to you. Thank you for telling me. I wish I had known sooner."

Eli felt a wave of relief wash over him. He hadn't realized how much he had needed to say those words until now. By sharing his feelings, he felt lighter, like a weight had been lifted. And he noticed something else—he felt closer to Lila, as if their friendship had deepened simply because he had been honest about how he felt.

Lila reached out and gave him a gentle hug. "You know, Eli, I think it's really brave that you shared that with me. It means a lot."

Eli smiled, feeling his heart fill with gratitude. Aspen's lesson was already proving itself true. Honesty had brought him closer to his friend, building a bond of trust and understanding. He knew he wanted to keep practicing this, to show up as his true self in all his relationships.

As he left Lila's house, he felt a new confidence blossoming within him, a strength that came from knowing he could be honest, even when it was hard. He thought about Aspen's lesson, about how honesty allowed him to share his burdens and find peace. He felt grateful for the tree's wisdom, knowing that this was a gift he would carry with him, not just today, but in all his future friendships and connections.

Walking through the park on his way home, Eli noticed the world around him with a renewed clarity. The trees, the grass, the sky—all of it seemed more vibrant, as if honesty had opened his eyes to a deeper, more colorful world. He thought about how honesty was like sunlight, illuminating everything it touched, revealing the beauty that sometimes hid in shadow.

Chapter 8: A Lesson from the Tree of Humility

Eli's heart brimmed with the wisdom he had gathered from each Wish Tree, each lesson like a precious stone he carried within him. Yet, he knew that his journey with the Wish Trees was far from over. With every visit to the grove, he felt himself growing in ways he hadn't imagined. The world seemed to open up with new colors, textures, and emotions, each visit teaching him a different way to see, feel, and understand.

One bright afternoon, Eli found himself drawn once again to the park. As he walked along the familiar paths, he felt a peaceful energy settle over him. He wondered what the next lesson might be, though he had learned not to guess or rush. Instead, he let the trees guide him, each one calling him when he was ready to learn. Today, he felt calm and open, ready to receive whatever the grove had to offer.

As he entered the grove, his eyes were drawn to a tree that stood a little off to the side, not as tall or as bright as the others, but with an undeniable presence. This tree's bark was smooth and light-colored, its branches strong yet modest, reaching out without stretching too high. The tree held itself with a kind of quiet grace, its leaves soft and green, swaying gently in the breeze. Eli sensed something different about this tree. It was neither grand nor bold, yet it had a beauty that drew him in.

He approached and placed his hand on the tree's cool bark, feeling a gentle hum of energy, calm and balanced. A voice began to speak, calm and kind, filled with warmth and a quiet strength.

"Hello, Eli," the voice said softly. "I am Willow, the Tree of Humility. I am here to teach you the beauty of humility, a quality that brings peace to the heart and harmony to our relationships with others. Humility is a gift, Eli, a way of seeing the world without putting oneself above or below others."

Eli thought about this, feeling curious yet uncertain. Humility was a word he had heard before, but he wasn't entirely sure what it meant. Was it about being humble, about not bragging or showing off? Willow seemed to sense his questions and continued, as if gently guiding his thoughts.

"Humility, Eli, is not about pretending to be less or making oneself small. It is about understanding that we are all part of a larger whole. Every person, every tree, every creature has a role to play, each one bringing its own beauty and purpose. Humility allows us to see the value in others without diminishing our own."

Eli felt a soft warmth bloom in his chest. Willow's words resonated with him, like a quiet melody that made him feel at peace. He thought about how often he had felt the need to prove himself, to be noticed or praised, and he realized that sometimes he had put too much focus on himself. Willow's lesson seemed to be about seeing beyond his own wants and needs, understanding that everyone around him was valuable in their own unique way.

Willow's gentle voice continued, "True humility helps us to listen, to appreciate the strengths and wisdom of others. It allows us to learn from those around us, to see that everyone has something to teach us. Humility reminds us that while we may have gifts, so does everyone else, and by recognizing their worth, we become richer, kinder, and more compassionate."

Eli thought about his friends, about times when he had wanted to be the best or have the last word, times when he had overlooked the strengths of others in his eagerness to be seen. Willow's lesson was opening his eyes to the beauty of simply listening, of being present without seeking to outshine anyone else. He felt a quiet understanding settle within him, a sense that humility wasn't about losing himself, but rather about connecting with others in a deeper, more genuine way.

Willow seemed to sense Eli's understanding and spoke again. "Humility also means accepting help when it's offered, Eli. It's easy to think we must do everything on our own, but humility reminds us that sometimes, the greatest strength is found in letting others support us. Just as the branches of trees lean on each other for balance, so can we lean on others for help, knowing it does not make us any less."

Eli reflected on this, remembering times when he had tried to do things alone, refusing help even when he felt overwhelmed. He realized that accepting help required a certain humility, a willingness to admit that he didn't have to be perfect or handle everything by himself. Willow's words filled him with a sense of relief, as if a weight had been lifted. He understood now that accepting help didn't make him weaker; it allowed him to grow and learn, connected to those around him.

Willow's leaves rustled softly, and the tree's voice filled his mind once more. "There is a quiet joy in humility, Eli, a peace that comes from knowing that we are enough as we are, without needing to prove it. Humility allows us to appreciate our own strengths and gifts without comparing them to others. It allows us to see that everyone's light shines in a unique way, and that each light contributes to the beauty of the world."

Eli felt a wave of gratitude for Willow's wisdom, realizing that humility wasn't about becoming less, but about celebrating the worth of everyone, including himself, without pride or arrogance. Willow had shown him that true strength lay in recognizing the value of others while still honoring his own worth.

With a calm smile, Eli thanked Willow, feeling lighter and more at peace than ever before. As he left the grove, he noticed a group of younger kids playing nearby, trying to build a small tower with blocks but struggling as the blocks kept toppling over. In the past, he might have stepped in right away, eager to show them how it was done, to be the "hero" of the moment. But today, he paused, watching quietly.

Instead of taking over, he offered to help, guiding them without trying to take the lead. He showed them a trick to keep the blocks steady and encouraged them to work together. As the tower grew, he saw the joy on their faces, the pride they felt in what they had built together. Eli felt a quiet satisfaction, knowing he had helped without seeking praise or recognition. It felt even better than being the hero.

Chapter 9: Discovering the Tree of Friendship

Eli's experiences with the Wish Trees had filled him with wonder, each tree offering him insights he hadn't expected. Each lesson was like a hidden path in the forest of his mind, leading him toward a deeper understanding of himself and the world around him. Today, as he made his way to the grove, he wondered what kind of lesson would await him this time. Friendship was a word that had always felt warm and familiar, yet he sensed there was more to it than just playing games or sharing stories.

As he stepped into the grove, he noticed a tree that seemed different from the others. It wasn't the tallest or the grandest, but it exuded an inviting energy that made Eli feel as though he were being welcomed with open arms. The tree's bark was smooth and a rich chestnut color, and its branches stretched wide, almost as if they were offering a gentle embrace. Eli felt a comfort in this tree's presence that he couldn't quite describe. Without hesitating, he approached, placing his hand on the warm bark, feeling the life and warmth radiating from within.

The tree's voice reached out to him, gentle and cheerful, like the laughter of an old friend. "Hello, Eli," it greeted him warmly. "I am Linden, the Tree of Friendship. I hold the gift of connection, the understanding that true friendship is a bond built on kindness, respect, and shared moments. Friendship is not simply about having fun; it is about supporting each other through life's ups and downs."

Eli felt a rush of excitement as he listened, eager to understand what Linden had to teach him. Friendship was something he cherished, but he hadn't thought much about its deeper meaning. It was a word he often used but hadn't fully explored. Linden's words seemed to promise that today would reveal something precious, a new understanding of what it meant to be a true friend.

"Friendship is like the branches of a tree," Linden continued, "stretching out, growing together, intertwining to create a shelter from the storms of life. A true friend offers both support and space, standing by us without overshadowing who we are. Friendship is a gift we give and receive, nurturing it with kindness, honesty, and patience."

Eli closed his eyes, absorbing Linden's words. He thought about his friends, Lila and Max, and all the times they had shared—moments of laughter, games, and adventures. Yet, he realized that true friendship had moments of challenge as well, times when they had to show patience, understanding, or forgiveness. Linden seemed to be telling him that friendship wasn't just about the fun times but about standing by each other, especially when things weren't easy.

Linden seemed to sense his thoughts and continued, "Friendship means giving and taking in equal measure, Eli. It means listening, really listening, to the needs of your friends. Sometimes, it means sharing your own heart, and other times, it means being there to hold space for someone else's feelings. True friends help each other grow, allowing each other to be who they truly are."

Eli thought about times when he had been impatient or distracted, not fully listening to his friends. He recalled moments when he had been so eager to share his own stories that he hadn't given his friends a chance to speak. He felt a gentle nudge of realization from Linden, reminding him that friendship was a dance of giving and receiving, of being present for others just as they were present for him.

Just then, Linden's branches swayed, and Eli felt a small, soft leaf drift down into his hand. It was heart-shaped, and he couldn't help but smile at how fitting it was for a lesson about friendship. Holding the leaf, he felt a warmth fill his chest, a sense of gratitude for his friends and the memories they had created together. He thought about ways he could be a better friend, ways he could show his friends that he valued them.

"Eli," Linden's voice gently pulled him back, "a true friend also learns to forgive and let go. Friendships will have their moments of disagreement and misunderstanding. There will be times when words are spoken in haste or feelings get hurt. But holding onto grudges builds walls between friends, while forgiveness builds bridges that bring hearts closer together."

Eli thought back to a recent argument he had with Max. It had been about something small, just a game they were playing, but it had left them both feeling hurt and distant. Eli realized that he had been holding onto that feeling, letting it sit in his heart like a heavy stone. He hadn't forgiven Max completely, even though the issue seemed trivial now. Linden's words encouraged him to let go of that weight, to choose forgiveness over pride. He understood now that forgiving his friends was a way to keep the friendship healthy and strong.

Linden continued, its voice filled with gentle wisdom. "Friendship also requires courage, Eli. Sometimes, being a true friend means standing up for each other, even when it's hard. It means speaking up when something feels wrong, not because you want to control or criticize, but because you care. True friends encourage each other to be their best selves, offering gentle guidance with kindness and respect."

Eli felt a swell of courage within him, understanding that being a friend wasn't always easy or comfortable. He thought of moments when he had seen someone mistreat his friends and hadn't known how to respond. He realized now that friendship sometimes meant having the courage to speak up, to protect each other's well-being. It meant supporting each other, not just with words, but with actions, showing up for one another when it mattered most.

Linden seemed to sense his newfound understanding and spoke once more. "Friendship, like any growing thing, needs care and attention. It is not something we can neglect or take for granted. Just as I need sunlight, water, and nurturing to thrive, so too do friendships need time, effort, and kindness to flourish. A true friend remembers to check in, to offer a listening ear or a helping hand, even when life becomes busy."

Eli thought about times he had forgotten to check in on his friends, especially when he was busy or distracted. He realized that being a friend was an ongoing effort, a commitment to nurture the bond they shared. Friendship wasn't something to take for granted; it was something to cherish and protect, just like a precious gift.

The heart-shaped leaf in his hand seemed to glow with meaning now, a symbol of all that Linden had shared. Eli felt grateful, not only for Linden's wisdom but also for the friendships in his life, each one a treasure he would hold close. Linden had shown him that true friendship was more than just playing and laughing together. It was a bond built on kindness, patience, forgiveness, and support. It was a gift he could give as much as he could receive.

Chapter 10: The Tree of Respect

Eli awoke on Saturday morning feeling a deep sense of calm, as if the world itself had slowed down just for him. The sky was a soft shade of blue, and the early morning sunlight poured through his window, filling his room with a gentle glow. He thought about his recent lessons from the Wish Trees, each one filling his heart with a different kind of warmth and understanding. Today, he felt drawn once again to the grove, wondering what new wisdom awaited him.

As he walked through the park, Eli noticed the people around him—each person moving with their own purpose, their own thoughts and dreams. He realized that everyone had a story, a journey as unique as his own. It was a simple thought, but it made the world feel a little larger and more beautiful.

When he entered the grove, Eli sensed a quiet strength in the air, a feeling that this lesson would be one of depth and importance. His eyes were drawn to a tall, graceful tree with smooth, silvery bark that caught the light in a way that made it seem almost alive. Its branches reached high, stretching with a quiet elegance, and its leaves shimmered with a soft green hue. Eli felt a calm energy emanating from the tree, a presence that felt both wise and kind.

He approached the tree and placed his hand on its bark, feeling its cool, smooth surface. A steady, gentle voice filled his mind, wrapping around him like a comforting embrace.

"Hello, Eli," the voice said with a serene strength. "I am Cedar, the Tree of Respect. My roots run deep, reminding me of the value of each life around me. I am here to teach you about respect, a gift that allows us to see the worth in every being and honor the unique path each one walks."

Eli felt a spark of curiosity. Respect was something he had often been told to show—respect for his elders, his friends, his teachers—but he realized that he didn't fully understand what it meant on a deeper level. Cedar's voice was gentle but firm, as if guiding him toward an understanding that would reach far beyond what he knew.

"Respect is more than politeness, Eli," Cedar continued. "It is a recognition of the value that each person, each creature, and each part of the world holds. It means seeing others not as less or more, but as unique beings with their own experiences, thoughts, and dreams. True respect allows us to embrace differences, to see diversity as a strength that enriches our lives."

Eli listened, feeling a new understanding begin to bloom within him. He had always thought of respect as something one showed to those in authority, but Cedar was teaching him that respect was about seeing everyone as valuable, regardless of age, role, or status. He thought about his friends and family, his teachers, and even strangers he saw in the park, realizing that each of them held a unique value, a story of their own.

Cedar seemed to sense his thoughts and spoke again. "Respect also means listening with an open heart, Eli. It is easy to hear words, but true respect requires us to listen beyond what is spoken, to understand others' perspectives, even when they differ from our own. When we listen with respect, we allow others to be seen and heard, strengthening the bonds between us."

Eli thought about times when he had been quick to judge or dismiss the ideas of others, focusing more on his own thoughts than on truly understanding those around him. Cedar's words helped him realize that listening with respect meant putting aside his own assumptions and being open to learning from others, no matter who they were.

"Respect is also about honoring boundaries," Cedar continued, its voice calm yet unwavering. "Each person, like each tree, has roots and branches that define their space. Respect means understanding these boundaries and allowing others the freedom to grow in their own way, without imposing our own expectations upon them."

Eli considered this, feeling a wave of insight. He thought about how, at times, he had expected others to act a certain way or share his opinions, not realizing that everyone had their own path and their own way of seeing the world. Cedar's lesson was showing him that respect meant letting others be themselves, without trying to change or control them.

The tree's branches swayed gently, as if affirming Eli's understanding. Cedar's voice continued, soft yet powerful. "True respect, Eli, allows us to stand in awe of the world around us, appreciating each part for its own unique beauty. It means not taking others for granted, but rather seeing the gifts they bring into our lives."

Eli felt a deep gratitude for Cedar's words, a gratitude that made the world feel both larger and more connected. He thought about the people in his life, the friends who shared their laughter, the teachers who shared their knowledge, even the animals in the park that brought life and movement to the landscape. Each one was a part of his world, each one bringing something unique and valuable.

Cedar seemed to feel his gratitude, and its voice filled his mind once more. "Respect also means respecting ourselves, Eli. When we recognize our own worth, our own strengths, we are better able to see the value in others. Self-respect is the foundation that allows us to stand tall, to offer our best selves to the world."

Eli thought about times when he had doubted himself, when he had felt as if he wasn't enough. Cedar's words reminded him that self-respect was not about pride but about honoring his own journey, his own growth, and recognizing that he, too, had a place and a purpose in the world.

With a calm, steady voice, Cedar offered one final thought. "Respect, Eli, is a way of living. It is a path of kindness, understanding, and humility. It invites us to see the world with gentle eyes, to cherish every being for the light they bring. When we walk with respect, we walk in harmony with the world around us, and we bring peace to our hearts and to the hearts of others."

Chapter 11: The Tree of Kindness in Action

As a new day began, Eli's heart full of excitement for the day ahead. Over the past few weeks, his visits to the grove had given him a sense of purpose and understanding that he hadn't known before. Each lesson from the Wish Trees felt like a new piece of a puzzle, helping him see the world and himself more clearly. Today, he had a feeling that he would learn something truly special, something that might be simple yet powerful.

After breakfast, he walked briskly to the park, his steps quick with anticipation. As he made his way to the grove, he passed by children playing, families walking together, and people quietly reading on benches. He noticed the laughter, the joy, and even the quiet moments of peace, and he felt a part of all of it, as if he were carrying a small piece of magic from the Wish Trees in his heart wherever he went.

When he reached the grove, Eli took a deep breath, letting the calming energy of the trees wash over him. He felt as though he was stepping into a world where time slowed down, where he could simply be. Today, his eyes were drawn to a tree that was different from any he had seen before. This tree wasn't particularly tall or wide, but it was covered in delicate, soft-looking leaves that almost shimmered with a gentle golden light. The tree seemed to radiate warmth and gentleness, an inviting presence that made Eli feel instantly comfortable.

He approached and placed his hand on the bark, feeling its smoothness. As he closed his eyes, a gentle voice filled his mind, warm and light like a soft breeze.

"Welcome, Eli," the voice said with a kindness that felt like a hug. "I am Olive, the Tree of Kindness. I am here to show you that kindness is not just a feeling but an action, a way of living that brings light to others and fills your own heart with peace."

Eli smiled, feeling the warmth of Olive's words settle within him. He had always known that kindness was important; his parents often reminded him to be kind to others. But Olive's words made him curious, as if there was something more to kindness than he had ever realized.

"Kindness, Eli, is more than polite words or good manners," Olive continued. "It is about seeing the needs of others and acting with a generous heart. It can be as simple as a smile or as grand as helping someone in need, but the essence of kindness is always the same: it is love in action, a choice to make the world a little brighter."

Eli thought about Olive's words, realizing that kindness was not just something he felt but something he could actively do. He thought about times when he had seen someone who looked lonely or sad and hadn't known what to say. Now, he wondered if kindness could be as simple as sitting with someone, offering a smile, or sharing a comforting word.

Olive seemed to sense his thoughts and spoke again. "Kindness is powerful, Eli. It doesn't always need to be big or noticeable. Sometimes, the smallest acts of kindness make the biggest difference. When you help someone carry a heavy bag, listen when they need to talk, or share your joy with others, you are spreading kindness. Each act, no matter how small, creates a ripple that can grow into waves of change."

Eli closed his eyes, letting Olive's words sink in. He imagined the world filled with ripples of kindness, each one growing and connecting, reaching people near and far. It was a beautiful thought, a reminder that even one small action could bring happiness to others.

Feeling inspired, Eli asked, "How can I be more kind, Olive? How do I know when someone needs kindness?"

The tree's voice was soft, almost like a whisper. "Kindness begins with noticing, Eli. It means looking around, paying attention to the people and the world around you. Sometimes, you may see someone who is struggling, or someone who is alone. Other times, kindness is simply sharing a moment of joy, offering a laugh, or brightening someone's day. The world is full of moments to be kind if you open your heart and look closely."

Eli felt a tingling sense of excitement, as if Olive had given him a special mission. He thought about how he could start noticing these small moments, finding ways to spread kindness in his daily life. It wasn't about being perfect or doing something grand; it was about being present and open to the needs of others, even if it was just for a brief moment.

Olive continued, her voice filled with warmth. "Remember, Eli, that kindness also includes kindness toward yourself. Sometimes, we can be too hard on ourselves, thinking we must be perfect or always do things right. But true kindness means treating yourself with the same compassion you would show to a friend. Being kind to yourself allows you to give more freely to others without feeling empty."

Eli thought about times when he had been hard on himself, criticizing his mistakes or feeling frustrated when things didn't go as planned. Olive's words made him realize that being kind to himself was just as important as being kind to others. It was a way to fill his own heart so that he could give more openly and generously.

As he stood there, Olive's branches swayed gently, and a soft, golden leaf drifted down, landing in his hand. Eli held it carefully, feeling its warmth, as if it were a reminder of the kindness Olive had shared. He thanked Olive, promising to carry this lesson in his heart.

As he left the grove, he looked around, determined to find small moments to be kind. It wasn't long before he saw an opportunity. On his way through the park, he noticed an elderly man struggling to reach for a book that had fallen from a bench. Eli approached him, smiling as he bent down to pick up the book and handed it back to the man.

"Thank you, young man," the man said with a smile that made Eli's heart feel light.

"It was no problem," Eli replied, feeling a quiet joy in knowing he had helped, even if it was something small. He walked away feeling that Olive's lesson was already becoming a part of him, guiding him in his actions.

As he continued his walk, Eli saw a young child looking lonely on a swing, watching the other children play but not joining them. Remembering Olive's words, he walked over and gave the child a warm smile.

"Hi! Would you like to play together?" he asked gently.

The child's face lit up, and they nodded eagerly. They spent the next few minutes laughing and playing, and Eli felt his heart swell with happiness, knowing that he had brought a little joy to someone else. Olive had been right—kindness could be as simple as sharing a moment, creating ripples of happiness that reached far beyond what he could see.

By the time he returned home, Eli's heart felt full. He thought about all the small ways he could continue to be kind, from helping his parents with chores to listening to his friends when they needed support. He realized that kindness wasn't something he had to plan; it was something he could do naturally, whenever he saw an opportunity.

Chapter 12: The Tree of Forgiveness

Eli set off toward the grove with a sense of purpose in his step. Over the past weeks, each lesson from the Wish Trees had woven itself into his heart, creating a foundation of wisdom he knew would stay with him forever. Each tree had shown him a way to connect more deeply with himself and the people around him, and he felt grateful for every moment spent learning in their presence. Today, however, there was a different feeling within him—a sense of heaviness, like a small stone resting in his chest. He couldn't quite put his finger on what it was, but he hoped the Wish Trees would help him find clarity.

As he entered the grove, he took a deep breath, the familiar earthy scent of the trees calming him. The world felt soft and quiet here, and he felt safe to open his heart to whatever lesson awaited him. His eyes were drawn to a tree standing gracefully to the left of the grove. This tree was neither tall nor wide, but it had a presence that was both gentle and strong, like the embrace of a friend after a long day. Its bark was smooth, a warm, pale shade of gray, and its branches spread wide, creating a canopy that felt welcoming and peaceful.

Eli approached the tree, placing his hand on its bark. As he did, he felt a warmth radiate through him, a kindness that seemed to ease the tension he hadn't realized he was carrying. A soft voice filled his mind, gentle and soothing, like a whisper on the wind.

"Hello, Eli," the voice said with a warmth that made him feel immediately at ease. "I am Magnolia, the Tree of Forgiveness. My gift is to help those who carry heavy burdens in their hearts, to let go of past hurts and find peace within themselves. Forgiveness is a path to healing, Eli, one that brings freedom and lightness to those willing to walk it."

Eli felt a shiver of understanding. Forgiveness. It was a word he had heard many times, but he had never truly thought about what it meant or how it felt. The stone-like weight in his chest seemed to stir as Magnolia spoke, and he began to wonder if he was holding onto something that needed to be released. He thought about times when he had felt hurt or disappointed, moments when he had felt wronged but hadn't known how to let go of those feelings.

"Forgiveness, Eli," Magnolia continued, her voice calm and wise, "is a way of letting go of the pain that others may have caused, intentionally or unintentionally. It is not about forgetting or pretending the hurt didn't happen, but rather choosing not to let it weigh you down. Forgiveness is a gift you give yourself, freeing your heart from anger and resentment."

Eli felt a mix of emotions as he listened. Forgiving sounded simple, yet there was a part of him that felt hesitant. He thought about a moment when he had felt betrayed by a friend who had shared something personal he had trusted them to keep secret. The sting of that memory made his heart ache, and he realized that he had been holding onto that pain, letting it cloud his feelings about his friend. The idea of forgiving felt challenging, almost as if he would be saying that what had happened didn't matter. But Magnolia's voice gently pulled him back, as if sensing his thoughts.

"Forgiveness does not mean excusing someone's actions or pretending that nothing happened, Eli. It is simply a choice to release the hold that pain has on your heart. When we hold onto anger, it creates a heaviness within us, like a stone that grows with each day we cling to it. Forgiveness allows us to let go of that stone, freeing our hearts to feel joy and love again."

Eli thought about this, feeling a glimmer of understanding. Magnolia was right—his hurt had felt like a weight, something he carried with him even when he didn't think about it directly. Letting go sounded like a release, a chance to feel light again. But he wondered how he could forgive when part of him still felt the sting of betrayal.

Magnolia's voice softened, her tone filled with empathy. "Forgiveness is a journey, Eli, one that takes time and patience. It may not happen all at once, and that's okay. Each small step you take toward letting go brings you closer to peace. Forgiveness is like a tree that grows slowly, its roots digging deep as it reaches toward the light. Trust that each step, no matter how small, is part of that growth."

Eli felt comforted by Magnolia's words. She was telling him that forgiveness didn't have to be a single, magical moment. It was a process, a decision he could make over and over until the pain softened and he felt free. The image of a tree growing steadily toward the light made him feel hopeful, as if forgiving his friend could be something gentle and natural.

As he stood there, a memory surfaced—an argument he had had with his sister just a few days ago. They had both said things they didn't mean, and since then, they had been avoiding each other, each too stubborn to apologize. Eli hadn't realized how much that argument had been weighing on him until now, and he felt a surge of sadness mixed with guilt. He wanted to forgive her, to let go of the anger and move forward, but he hadn't known how. Magnolia's lesson seemed to hold the answer.

Magnolia continued, her voice as calming as a lullaby. "Forgiveness, Eli, is a gift not only for those who have hurt us but also for ourselves. It allows us to find peace, to move forward without carrying the weight of the past. Forgiving someone does not mean allowing them to hurt you again; it simply means you are choosing to free your heart."

Eli felt a newfound resolve to try. He closed his eyes, imagining the pain he felt toward his friend and his sister as stones resting in his hands. He imagined setting those stones down at the base of Magnolia, letting the tree take them in, like seeds planted in the earth. He felt a small, comforting release as he visualized this, as if he had made space in his heart for something lighter, something brighter.

As he opened his eyes, he saw a soft, white flower fall from Magnolia's branches, landing gently in his hand. The flower's petals were delicate, almost translucent, and Eli felt it was a symbol of the forgiveness Magnolia had helped him begin. He knew he hadn't fully let go of his hurt, but this was a first step, a beginning that would allow him to grow.

With Magnolia's wisdom fresh in his heart, Eli left the grove, feeling both lighter and stronger. He decided to put his new understanding of forgiveness into action, beginning with his sister. When he got home, he found her in the living room, reading. Taking a deep breath, he approached her.

"Hey," he said softly, "I'm sorry about our argument the other day. I shouldn't have said some of those things. Can we forgive each other and move on?"

His sister looked up, surprise mixed with relief in her eyes. She nodded, and they shared a small smile, the tension between them melting away. Eli felt a sense of peace settle over him, a warmth that reminded him of Magnolia's gentle presence.

Chapter 13: Celebrating the Tree of Unity

Eli woke up to the sound of birds chirping outside his window, the morning sunlight spilling into his room like warm honey. He lay there for a moment, reflecting on all he had learned from the Wish Trees so far. Each lesson felt like a gift, one that had slowly shaped him, helping him see the world through new eyes. Today, he felt an unfamiliar excitement, a sense that something extraordinary awaited him. The air felt charged with possibility, and he couldn't wait to discover what the trees had in store.

After breakfast, he made his way to the park, his steps quick with anticipation. The park was bustling with life as families and friends gathered, talking and laughing, and children played freely. Eli watched them, noticing how everyone seemed to be part of a larger story. He felt a deep appreciation for the beauty in people coming together, each person adding something unique to the scene.

As he approached the grove, he noticed a tree that seemed to glow with a gentle, inviting energy. This tree was different from any he had seen before. Its bark was a blend of colors—soft browns, grays, and greens that seemed to flow together, as if each color was connected to the other. The branches stretched wide and intertwined with the neighboring trees, creating a canopy that felt almost like a shelter, a place where differences could come together in harmony. Eli felt drawn to it immediately, sensing that this tree held a powerful lesson.

Placing his hand on the smooth, cool bark, he felt a surge of warmth and unity, as if the tree were enveloping him in an invisible embrace. A deep, resonant voice filled his mind, steady and kind.

"Welcome, Eli," the tree said in a tone that felt both ancient and timeless. "I am Banyan, the Tree of Unity. I am here to show you that we are all connected, each person, each creature, each leaf, and stone, woven together in a web of life. Unity is the thread that binds us, allowing us to stand stronger together than we ever could alone."

Eli listened, feeling a thrill of recognition. Unity was a word he had heard before, but he had never truly understood its depth. As he stood with Banyan, he felt the tree's message within his heart—a reminder that each person and each living thing was part of something greater, connected by invisible threads that were both strong and delicate.

"Unity," Banyan continued, "is about seeing the beauty in diversity, understanding that our differences are not barriers but bridges. Each person, each being, has something unique to offer, something only they can bring. When we come together, sharing our strengths and accepting our differences, we create a harmony that is greater than any one part alone."

Eli thought about Banyan's words, feeling a deep respect for the idea that differences were to be celebrated, not feared. He realized that every person he knew—his friends, family, teachers, even people he saw only in passing—was like a unique note in a song, each contributing to a melody that was richer and fuller than any single note could create alone.

Banyan seemed to sense Eli's understanding and continued with a gentle wisdom. "Unity is not always easy, Eli. There will be times when people disagree, when differences create misunderstandings. But true unity is about finding common ground, learning to see from each other's perspectives, and working together to overcome challenges. Unity requires both strength and kindness, a willingness to stand together despite our differences."

Eli thought about times when he had disagreed with his friends, moments when their differences had made him feel distant or misunderstood. He realized that true unity didn't mean everyone was the same; it meant valuing each other's unique qualities and finding ways to come together. It was about building bridges where there might be gaps, understanding that each person's view was shaped by their own experiences.

As Banyan's branches swayed gently in the breeze, Eli felt as though the tree was sharing its strength with him, helping him see unity as a powerful force. Banyan's voice filled his mind once more, warm and steady. "Unity also means standing together in difficult times, supporting each other when the road becomes rough. Just as my branches intertwine with the other trees, giving support and shelter, so too can we lean on each other, knowing that together, we are stronger than we are alone."

Eli felt a surge of gratitude for Banyan's words, realizing that unity was about more than just harmony; it was about support, about being there for one another in times of need. He thought about his friends, about how they had always been there for each other, through both the happy times and the challenging ones. Unity wasn't just a feeling—it was an action, a commitment to hold each other up.

Banyan seemed to feel Eli's gratitude and continued. "Unity is a gift we give to each other, Eli. It is the choice to see each other as part of a larger whole, to recognize that when we help others, we are also helping ourselves. Unity allows us to celebrate both our individual strengths and the strength we gain from standing together."

Eli closed his eyes, imagining the connections that Banyan spoke of, the invisible threads that tied him to his friends, his family, and even the people he didn't know well. He saw each person as a part of a larger picture, each thread adding to the strength and beauty of the whole. It was a comforting thought, one that made him feel both grounded and uplifted.

When he opened his eyes, he noticed a small gathering of people nearby—a group of children were attempting to put together a large puzzle, each piece different but essential to the whole. The children were struggling, and a few of them were beginning to argue about where each piece should go. Eli felt a nudge from Banyan, as if the tree were encouraging him to bring the lesson of unity to life.

Inspired, Eli walked over to the group. He noticed that each child had their own idea about how the puzzle should be put together, and they were growing frustrated, their voices rising as they tried to make themselves heard. Eli took a deep breath, remembering Banyan's lesson about unity, and approached them calmly.

"Hey, everyone," he said with a smile. "Why don't we each try to find one piece that fits? If we all work together, I think we can complete the puzzle faster."

The children looked at him, their frustration softening as they considered his suggestion. They nodded, each taking a piece and looking for where it might fit, helping each other find matches along the way. Slowly, the puzzle began to take shape, each piece connecting to the next, forming a beautiful picture that none of them could have completed alone.

Chapter 14: The Tree of Hope

Eli woke up that morning with a feeling he couldn't quite place, a sensation that hovered somewhere between excitement and calm. It felt like the dawn itself held something special, an invitation to see the world through fresh eyes. After all his lessons with the Wish Trees, he had begun to notice that each day carried its own kind of magic, a new way to see, feel, and understand things. He could only imagine what today's lesson might hold, and the curiosity pulled him out of bed and out the door with a quiet eagerness.

The park was still and peaceful when he arrived, the early light softening the landscape into shades of green and gold. The trees stood silent and strong, watching over the world with a timeless patience. As Eli walked through the grove, his eyes landed on a tree he hadn't noticed before. It was slender and graceful, its trunk a warm, silvery color that seemed to shimmer faintly in the morning light. The leaves were a gentle, silvery green, like small drops of sunlight caught in delicate branches. This tree exuded a sense of calm and encouragement, as if it were offering a gentle hand, promising that everything would be alright.

Eli felt drawn to it, sensing that this tree held something important, something he needed even if he didn't know why. Placing his hand on the bark, he felt a rush of warmth and comfort, like being wrapped in a blanket on a chilly evening. A soft, reassuring voice filled his mind, steady and clear.

"Hello, Eli," the voice said, filled with a kind strength. "I am Willow, the Tree of Hope. My gift is to remind those who feel weary or uncertain that there is always light, even in the darkest times. Hope is the promise of tomorrow, a belief in the possibilities that lie ahead, even when the path feels unclear."

Eli felt a thrill of recognition. Hope. It was a word that held a kind of quiet power, a strength that wasn't about might or force but about belief. Willow's words stirred something within him, like a small flame flickering to life. Hope was something he had always felt but never fully understood. In moments of doubt or fear, he had often felt a pull toward a brighter thought, a possibility that things would get better. He hadn't realized that this feeling had a name, that it was called hope.

Willow continued, her voice soft yet unwavering. "Hope is the ability to see beyond the present moment, to look forward with a belief that challenges can be overcome and that joy awaits. It is like a light that guides us, even when we feel lost or unsure."

Eli closed his eyes, letting Willow's words settle within him. He thought about times when he had felt uncertain or discouraged, when the world had seemed confusing or difficult. In those moments, he remembered feeling a spark, a sense that things could change for the better, even if he couldn't see exactly how. Willow was teaching him that this spark was hope, a small but powerful force that helped him keep going, even when he couldn't see the path ahead.

"Hope is not about ignoring challenges, Eli," Willow continued, as if sensing his thoughts. "It is about facing them with a heart that believes in possibility. Hope does not pretend that there is no darkness; it simply reminds us that light will return. It is a faith in the strength within us, a trust that we can overcome."

Eli felt a warmth spread through him, a sense of comfort that wrapped around him like a gentle embrace. Hope was not a way of ignoring life's difficulties, but a way of moving through them with courage. It was a way of looking beyond the shadows, knowing that sunlight was always waiting on the other side. He felt a growing strength within him, a reassurance that even the hardest days held the promise of something better.

Willow's voice softened, filling his heart with a quiet certainty. "Hope is also something we can give to others, Eli. Just as light can be shared, so can hope. A kind word, a gentle gesture, a reminder that we believe in them—these are ways to share hope, ways to lift others when they feel weary."

Eli thought about the people in his life, about friends who had struggled, family members who had faced challenges. He realized that each time he had offered support or encouragement, he had been sharing hope, giving them a glimpse of light in times of darkness. He thought of his friend Lila, who had recently been nervous about a big test at school. Eli had told her that he believed in her, that she was smart and capable. He hadn't known it then, but he had been offering her hope, a small reminder that she could face the challenge and succeed.

Willow continued, her voice like a steady heartbeat. "Hope is a gift we give ourselves and others, Eli. It reminds us that we are never truly alone, that there are always possibilities waiting for us, even if we cannot see them yet. Hope allows us to keep going, to trust in the journey, knowing that every step brings us closer to the light."

Eli felt a deep gratitude for Willow's words, a gratitude that filled him with a sense of purpose. He realized that hope was something he could carry within him, a light he could turn to whenever he felt unsure. And it was something he could share, a way to lift others and remind them that they, too, could find their way through difficult times.

As he stood there, absorbing Willow's lesson, he noticed a small group of children playing nearby. They were building a fort with sticks and leaves, their laughter ringing through the air like music. But he noticed one boy standing a bit apart, watching the others with a sad expression. Eli felt a tug in his heart, a nudge from Willow's lesson about sharing hope.

Walking over, Eli approached the boy with a friendly smile. "Hi," he said gently. "Would you like to join us? We could use some help with the fort."

The boy looked at him, a glimmer of hope lighting up his eyes. Slowly, he nodded, his face softening. Together, they joined the group, and soon the boy was laughing and working alongside the others, his earlier sadness forgotten. Eli felt a quiet joy knowing that he had offered the boy a small piece of hope, a reminder that he was welcome, that he could be part of something joyful.

Chapter 15: Learning from the Tree of Gratitude in Action

Eli got up that morning with a contented sigh, his mind filled with thoughts of the Wish Trees and all the lessons they had shared. Each tree's wisdom had added something precious to his heart, something that shaped the way he saw the world and the people in it. As he stretched and got ready for the day, he felt a special kind of excitement, a sense that today's lesson might be about something he could practice, something he could carry with him and share with others.

The morning air was cool as he made his way to the park, the sunlight filtering softly through the trees. Every step brought him closer to the grove, to the hidden world where the Wish Trees waited, each one with a unique message for those willing to listen. When he entered the grove, he felt a wave of warmth, a gentle welcome that wrapped around him like a favorite blanket.

His eyes were drawn to a tree standing quietly on the edge of the grove. It was a modest tree, not as tall as some of the others, but its branches were full and leafy, spreading wide as if to embrace the world around it. The bark was rough and textured, a deep, rich brown that felt solid and reassuring. Eli felt a calm energy radiating from this tree, a feeling of quiet appreciation and warmth. He walked over, placing his hand on the bark, and felt a gentle vibration, a peaceful hum that seemed to echo in his chest.

A calm, warm voice filled his mind, steady and soft like the murmur of leaves in a breeze. "Welcome, Eli," the voice said. "I am Oak, the Tree of Gratitude in Action. I am here to remind you that gratitude is more than a feeling; it is a way of living, a way to see and interact with the world. Gratitude is something that grows when we nurture it, becoming a light that brightens our lives and the lives of those around us."

Eli felt a flicker of recognition. Gratitude was a word he knew, something his parents had often encouraged him to practice. But Oak's words made him realize that gratitude wasn't just about saying "thank you" or feeling good about what he had. Oak was talking about gratitude as something much deeper, something active, that could shape the way he experienced every moment.

"Gratitude," Oak continued, "is more than appreciation; it is the choice to focus on the blessings in your life, even in moments of difficulty. It is the ability to see the beauty in small things, to be thankful for the simple gifts that surround you. When you live with gratitude, you open your heart to the world, finding joy even in unexpected places."

Eli closed his eyes, thinking about the small things he was grateful for—his family, his friends, the quiet beauty of the park, even the warmth of the sun on his face. Each thought filled him with a gentle warmth, a feeling that spread through him like the rays of the sun itself. He understood that gratitude wasn't something he only felt when something special happened; it was something he could practice every day, noticing and appreciating even the smallest joys.

"Living with gratitude also means sharing that joy with others," Oak continued. "When you express gratitude, you bring light into the world. It encourages others to see the good in their own lives, creating a cycle of appreciation and kindness. Gratitude grows when it is shared, turning a single feeling into a source of strength and connection."

Eli thought about times he had seen gratitude in action, moments when a kind word or a small act of appreciation had lifted someone's spirits. He remembered a time his friend Max had given him a hand-drawn card after Eli helped him with a difficult homework assignment. The card had been simple but heartfelt, and Eli had felt a deep appreciation, not just for the card itself but for the thought behind it. He realized that showing gratitude could be as simple as a kind gesture, something that created a bond between people, making them feel seen and valued.

Oak's branches seemed to sway gently, as if encouraging Eli to continue reflecting. "Gratitude is also a way to find peace, Eli," Oak said softly. "When you focus on what you have, rather than what you lack, you free yourself from the desire for more. You learn to appreciate the present moment, finding contentment and joy in the here and now."

Eli felt a sense of calm settle over him. He thought about times when he had wished for things he didn't have—a new toy, a special adventure, something exciting or different. But now he realized that by focusing on what he had, he could find a kind of quiet happiness, a contentment that came from truly seeing the richness of his life. He understood that gratitude wasn't just a feeling; it was a way of looking at the world, a way to see the abundance that was already there.

Feeling inspired, Eli asked, "How can I practice gratitude, Oak? How can I make it something I do every day?"

The tree's voice was warm and reassuring, like a gentle smile. "Begin by noticing, Eli. Take time each day to appreciate the blessings around you—the beauty of nature, the kindness of others, the warmth of home. Gratitude is like a garden; the more you tend to it, the more it grows, filling your heart with joy and peace. And remember, gratitude grows best when it is shared."

Eli thought about Oak's words, feeling a sense of purpose blossom within him. He could practice gratitude every day, making it a part of his life, a way of seeing the world. And he could share that gratitude with others, creating a ripple of appreciation that could brighten the lives of everyone around him.

As he left the grove, he looked for ways to put Oak's lesson into action. Walking through the park, he noticed a man sitting on a bench, looking downcast and tired. Remembering Oak's words about sharing gratitude, Eli felt a nudge to offer something kind, something that might bring a bit of light into the man's day.

Eli approached him, offering a gentle smile. "Hi," he said warmly. "Is everything okay? I just wanted to say that I hope you have a good day."

The man looked up, surprised but grateful, his face softening as he returned Eli's smile. "Thank you, young man. That's very kind of you," he said, his eyes brightening just a little.

Eli walked away, feeling a sense of warmth and satisfaction. It had been a small gesture, but he knew that it had made a difference, a small spark of kindness that might brighten the man's day.

As he continued through the park, he saw other moments for gratitude in action. He stopped to help a younger child who had dropped their toys, bending down to pick them up and hand them back with a smile. He paused to thank the park gardener, who was busy trimming bushes, for keeping the park so beautiful. Each act felt like a small celebration, a way of showing appreciation for the world around him.

Chapter 16: The Tree of Acceptance

Eli's new day began with a feeling of calmness and curiosity. The world outside his window was still and quiet, the morning sunlight painting everything in a soft golden glow. Each visit to the Wish Trees had filled his heart with a unique lesson, a new way to see and appreciate life. Today, as he prepared to return to the grove, he felt a sense of mystery, as if the lesson waiting for him would be something different, something he would carry with him for a long time.

The park was peaceful as he walked through, with only a few early birds going about their morning routines. As he entered the grove, he felt a familiar warmth surround him, a gentle welcome that made him feel at home. He let his gaze wander, wondering which tree would call to him today. His eyes landed on a tree he had never really noticed before. It was neither tall nor particularly striking; in fact, it looked a bit twisted, its branches curving in unexpected directions. Its leaves were a deep, rich green, but some were spotted with small, gentle imperfections. Yet, despite its unusual shape, the tree had a quiet beauty that was hard to ignore. Eli felt drawn to it, sensing that it held a lesson as unique as the tree itself.

Placing his hand on the tree's bark, he felt a rough texture, yet it was warm and solid, grounding him in the moment. A soft voice filled his mind, gentle and reassuring, carrying a wisdom that seemed to embrace him.

"Hello, Eli," the voice said with a kindness that felt like a warm breeze. "I am Juniper, the Tree of Acceptance. I am here to teach you about embracing things as they are, seeing the beauty in life's imperfections, and understanding that acceptance is a gift we give ourselves and others. Acceptance is not about giving up or settling; it is about finding peace with the reality of each moment, each person, each situation."

Eli listened closely, feeling a spark of recognition. Acceptance was a word he had heard before, but he had never thought about what it truly meant. Juniper's voice was calming, wrapping around him like a gentle hug. As he stood there, he realized that acceptance was about more than just agreeing with something; it was about understanding, respecting, and making peace with things that couldn't be changed.

"Acceptance," Juniper continued, "is about seeing the beauty in differences, in imperfections, and in things we may not fully understand. Just as each tree in this grove is unique, each person, each situation, and each challenge holds its own purpose. Acceptance allows us to appreciate the richness of life, to see that every twist and turn has its place in the world."

Eli thought about Juniper's words, letting them sink in. He thought about times when he had wished things were different, when he had wanted people to change or situations to go his way. He realized that sometimes he had resisted accepting things, feeling frustrated or disappointed when life didn't match his expectations. But Juniper's lesson was showing him a new way to see things, a way to find peace by embracing what was, rather than wishing for what could be.

Juniper's voice continued, soft and steady. "Acceptance does not mean you cannot hope or dream, Eli. It simply means understanding that there is beauty in what is, just as there is beauty in what might be. When you accept things as they are, you find freedom from the weight of expectation, allowing your heart to rest in the present moment."

Eli closed his eyes, letting Juniper's words settle in his heart. He thought about times he had been frustrated with himself, wishing he were different, or moments he had felt disappointed in others when they didn't act as he expected. He realized that by holding onto these expectations, he had sometimes missed the beauty of simply being, of allowing himself and others to be exactly as they were. Juniper was teaching him that acceptance was about letting go of the need to control, finding peace in what was real and present.

"Acceptance also means being kind to yourself, Eli," Juniper continued, sensing his thoughts. "It means understanding that you, too, are a part of the world's beauty, with all your strengths and weaknesses. When you accept yourself, you allow your heart to grow, to find joy in who you are without needing to change to fit anyone's expectations, not even your own."

Eli felt a warmth bloom in his chest, a sense of relief he hadn't realized he needed. He thought about the times he had been hard on himself, moments when he had felt like he wasn't enough, like he needed to be more or better in some way. Juniper's words were like a soothing balm, reminding him that he didn't need to be perfect to be worthy. Acceptance wasn't about changing himself; it was about seeing his own value, his own beauty, just as he was.

Juniper's voice filled his mind once more, gentle but filled with strength. "Acceptance is a way to connect with others, Eli. When you accept people as they are, with their differences and imperfections, you create a space for kindness and understanding. It allows you to see beyond the surface, to connect with the true essence of those around you. Acceptance is the foundation of compassion, a gift that builds bridges and brings people closer."

Eli thought about his friends and family, about moments when he had wanted them to act a certain way or share his perspective. He realized that acceptance meant letting go of those expectations, seeing them for who they were, not who he wished them to be. It was a way to honor their unique journeys, to appreciate them fully without trying to change them. He understood now that acceptance was a gift, a way to strengthen his relationships by seeing and appreciating others for exactly who they were.

As he stood there, Juniper's branches swayed gently in the breeze, and Eli felt a sense of peace wash over him. Acceptance wasn't about giving up or settling; it was about freeing his heart from the struggle of trying to control everything around him. It was a way to open his heart, to let life flow naturally, allowing him to find joy and peace in each moment, each person, each experience.

Feeling inspired, Eli thanked Juniper, the tree's wisdom filling him with a gentle courage to live with acceptance in his heart. As he left the grove, he noticed the world around him in a different light. Every person, every tree, every sound seemed richer, more vibrant, each part of life holding its own place in the grand design of the world.

Chapter 17: The Tree of Resilience

Eli awoke to the sound of rain tapping gently against his window, a steady, rhythmic patter that filled the morning with a quiet, reflective energy. It was the kind of day that made everything feel a little softer, a little more introspective. Over the past months, his visits to the Wish Trees had given him insights into kindness, patience, humility, and more, each lesson building upon the last. He had come to treasure the wisdom of the trees, knowing that each one carried a unique gift to share. Today, he felt a certain strength within him, a readiness for whatever lesson awaited him, even if he didn't yet know what it would be.

Eli pulled on his rain jacket and set off for the park, feeling the fresh, cool air on his face. The world around him seemed quieter than usual, as if the rain had wrapped everything in a gentle embrace. As he entered the grove, he took a deep breath, feeling the familiar warmth of the Wish Trees surround him, like a silent chorus welcoming him home. His eyes wandered, searching for the tree that would speak to him today.

Near the center of the grove stood a tree that seemed unlike any he had seen before. It was tall and sturdy, its trunk wide and deeply grooved, bearing the marks of years weathering countless storms. Its branches were thick and strong, some of them twisted and knotted in ways that suggested a resilience born of struggle. Despite its weathered appearance, the tree's leaves were vibrant and full, each one a rich shade of green that stood in defiance of the gray sky above. Eli felt an instant respect for this tree, sensing that it held a story of strength and perseverance.

He placed his hand on the rough bark, feeling a power that was both calming and energizing. A deep, resonant voice filled his mind, steady and unwavering, carrying a weight that felt like the wisdom of centuries.

"Hello, Eli," the voice greeted him, its tone warm but firm. "I am Chestnut, the Tree of Resilience. I am here to teach you about finding strength within yourself, even when times are tough. Resilience is the courage to keep going, the ability to bend but not break, to rise again no matter how many storms may come."

Eli felt a surge of recognition, an understanding that seemed to connect with a part of himself he hadn't fully explored. Resilience was a word he had heard before, but he hadn't thought much about what it really meant. Standing with Chestnut, he felt a new sense of purpose, as if he were being given a tool he might carry for a lifetime. He thought about moments when he had felt discouraged or uncertain, times when he had been tempted to give up or feel defeated. He realized that resilience was something he had always admired in others, yet he had never thought of it as something he could nurture within himself.

"Resilience," Chestnut continued, "is not about ignoring hardship or pretending things are easy. It is about facing challenges with a heart that believes in its own strength. Resilience allows you to grow through difficulty, to find a way forward even when the path is unclear."

Eli closed his eyes, letting Chestnut's words fill his mind. He thought about times when he had struggled with schoolwork or felt frustrated with things he couldn't change. He had often felt small in those moments, unsure of how to move past them. But Chestnut's lesson was opening his eyes to a different way of seeing things. Resilience wasn't about avoiding challenges or wishing they didn't exist; it was about learning to stand strong, even when life felt uncertain or difficult.

"Resilience means learning to adapt, Eli," Chestnut continued, his voice as steady as the tree itself. "It means bending with the wind, like branches that sway without breaking, finding new ways to grow even when the world around you changes. It is the ability to stay true to yourself, to hold on to your values and your dreams, even when things don't go as planned."

Eli felt a deep admiration for Chestnut's words, a sense of awe at the idea that resilience could be so powerful, so rooted in strength and flexibility. He thought about times when he had wanted things to stay the same, when he had resisted change because it made him feel uncertain. But Chestnut's words showed him that change didn't have to be something to fear. Resilience was about adapting, finding a way to grow no matter what the circumstances were. It was about trusting himself, knowing that he could navigate the unexpected.

"Resilience also means finding hope in difficult times," Chestnut said, his voice carrying a calm strength. "Even when things seem dark, resilience allows you to look for the light, to hold on to a sense of purpose that guides you through. It is about seeing each challenge as a step on your journey, an opportunity to learn and grow."

As Eli stood there, Chestnut's branches swayed gently, as if inviting him to embrace this strength within himself. He felt a new kind of confidence, a sense of peace that came from knowing he could face whatever life brought his way. Resilience wasn't about always being strong; it was about believing in his ability to rise, no matter how many times he fell.

Chapter 18: The Tree of Empathy

It was a crisp, cool morning when Eli woke up, the kind of day that felt fresh and inviting. The lessons he had learned from the Wish Trees felt like stepping stones, each one guiding him to a deeper understanding of himself and the world around him. Today, he felt an unfamiliar sense of anticipation, as if the grove was holding a lesson that he would need to carry forward in every part of his life. After getting ready, he set off for the park, excitement mixing with a calm curiosity.

The park was serene as he walked through it, the early light casting a gentle glow over the landscape. As he entered the grove, he felt a familiar warmth spread through him, a welcome that made him feel both safe and seen. He let his gaze drift over the trees, wondering which one would speak to him today. His eyes settled on a tall, graceful tree with soft, feathery leaves that seemed to sway gently, even in the stillness of the morning. Its trunk was smooth and light-colored, with intricate patterns that resembled a web connecting each part of the tree. Eli felt an immediate pull toward it, sensing that this tree held a lesson close to his heart.

Placing his hand on the bark, he felt a warmth radiate from within, a gentle pulse that seemed to echo with life. A soft, understanding voice filled his mind, a voice that carried both kindness and wisdom.

"Hello, Eli," the voice greeted him warmly. "I am Willow, the Tree of Empathy. I am here to teach you about seeing and feeling the world through the hearts of others. Empathy is the ability to connect deeply, to understand not just with your mind but with your heart. It is a gift that allows us to truly see each other, to offer kindness and support without judgment."

Eli listened, feeling a sense of recognition. Empathy was a word he knew, but he hadn't thought much about its true meaning. Willow's words made him realize that empathy wasn't just about knowing how someone else felt; it was about truly understanding, stepping into their world for a moment to see life as they did. He sensed that this lesson would show him a new way to connect, a way that would deepen his relationships with everyone around him.

"Empathy," Willow continued, her voice gentle and encouraging, "is about opening your heart to the feelings and experiences of others. It requires listening, not just with your ears but with your entire being. It is the choice to set aside your own thoughts for a moment, to be present with someone else in their joy, their pain, their struggles, or their dreams."

Eli closed his eyes, letting Willow's words sink in. He thought about times when he had listened to his friends, moments when they had shared their worries or their excitement. He realized that true empathy meant giving his full attention, really tuning in to what they were feeling, even if he didn't fully understand. It was about being there, not to fix or judge, but simply to understand and share in their experience.

"Empathy is like a bridge, Eli," Willow continued. "It connects us to others, helping us see that we are not so different from one another. Each person has their own story, their own challenges, and when you approach them with empathy, you build a bridge of understanding. It is a way to bring people closer, to create bonds that are strong and filled with kindness."

Eli thought about Willow's words, feeling a deep respect for the power of empathy. He thought about people he saw each day—his family, his friends, even strangers he passed on the street. Each person had their own story, their own thoughts and feelings, and he realized that empathy was a way to honor those stories, to see people for who they were beneath the surface. Willow's lesson was showing him that empathy was about more than just caring; it was a way of truly connecting, of seeing each person as a part of himself.

Willow's voice continued, filled with a calm, steady strength. "Empathy is also a gift to yourself, Eli. When you open your heart to

ELI AND THE WISH TREES

the experiences of others, you deepen your own understanding of the world. Empathy expands your heart, allowing you to feel more, to see more, and to live with a greater compassion for everyone around you."

Eli felt a warmth blossom in his chest, a sense of purpose growing within him. He understood now that empathy wasn't just something he gave to others; it was something that enriched his own life, helping him see the world with a broader, kinder perspective. Willow's words reminded him that empathy was a gift that flowed both ways, bringing understanding and kindness not only to others but also to himself.

"Sometimes, empathy means feeling pain," Willow said softly, as if reading his thoughts. "When we connect with others, we may feel their sadness, their struggles. But empathy is not about taking on their pain; it is about sharing it, offering comfort and support while keeping your own heart whole. Empathy requires strength, a balance of compassion and understanding, allowing you to stand with others without losing yourself."

Eli thought about times when he had seen his friends sad or hurt. He remembered feeling their pain, wanting to help but sometimes feeling overwhelmed by the intensity of it. Willow's words showed him that empathy wasn't about carrying someone else's burden entirely; it was about sharing it, offering support without losing his own inner strength. Empathy was a balance, a way to connect without becoming overwhelmed.

As he stood there, Willow's branches swayed gently in the breeze, and Eli felt a sense of peace wash over him. Empathy was a powerful force, one that required both courage and kindness. He understood now that it was a choice to see beyond his own world, to step into the shoes of others even when it was difficult. It was a way of living that made every relationship, every interaction, richer and more meaningful.

Feeling inspired, Eli thanked Willow, his heart filled with a new determination to live with empathy. As he left the grove, he looked around at the world in a different light, noticing the people he passed with a sense of curiosity and compassion. Each person he saw, he realized, had their own story, their own struggles and joys. Empathy was a way to honor those stories, to see people as they truly were, not just as they appeared.

That day, as he walked through the park, he noticed a young girl sitting alone on a bench, looking sad and lost in thought. Remembering Willow's lesson, he approached her gently, sitting down a few feet away to give her space. After a moment, he spoke softly, "Are you okay? Do you want to talk?"

The girl looked up, surprised but grateful. She nodded, her eyes filled with a sadness that Eli could feel even without knowing her story. She told him about her worries, her fears, and Eli listened, really listened, offering his presence without trying to fix or change anything. He simply shared in her moment, letting her feel seen and heard. He realized that empathy wasn't about having the right answers; it was about being there, fully and openly, creating a space where someone else could feel safe.

As they talked, Eli felt a deep sense of connection, a warmth that filled him with gratitude for Willow's lesson. When the girl finally smiled, he knew that his empathy had made a difference, offering her a small piece of comfort and understanding. It was a moment of pure connection, a bond that was built on kindness and understanding.

Chapter 19: The Tree of Patience

This day began with a soft light of dawn filtering through his window. The world outside seemed especially still, as if it were waiting for the day to begin. His heart felt peaceful, steady, and he took his time getting ready, savoring the quiet morning. Each of the Wish Trees had shared a unique lesson with him, and he had begun to see the world through new eyes. The lessons weren't always easy, but they felt like seeds planted in his heart, growing slowly and steadily with each passing day. Today, he sensed that the trees would teach him something essential, something he would need not just now but for his whole life.

When he arrived at the park, a soft breeze carried the scent of freshly cut grass and blooming flowers. The peacefulness of the morning made him feel grounded and open to whatever the trees had to share. As he walked through the grove, his eyes landed on a tree he hadn't noticed before. It stood alone, quiet and unassuming, its branches reaching out in graceful arcs. The bark was smooth and a soft, pale gray, and the tree's leaves were a deep, calm green that seemed to reflect the stillness of the moment. Eli felt drawn to this tree, sensing that it held a lesson that would require him to be fully present.

He placed his hand on the trunk, feeling the solidity of the tree beneath his fingers. A gentle, steady voice filled his mind, carrying a warmth that seemed to wrap around him like a blanket.

"Hello, Eli," the voice greeted him, its tone calm and comforting. "I am Cypress, the Tree of Patience. I am here to teach you about waiting with an open heart, about trusting in the timing of life. Patience is a quiet strength, a way of accepting life's rhythms, knowing that each moment has its own pace and purpose."

Eli felt a flicker of understanding, a sense that patience was something he needed to learn, though it wasn't always easy. He thought about moments when he had felt restless or frustrated, times when he had wanted things to happen quickly, without delay. Cypress's voice was soothing, a reminder that life didn't need to be rushed. He realized that patience was something he had often overlooked, seeing it as simply waiting, when perhaps it was something more.

"Patience, Eli," Cypress continued, "is about trusting that things will happen when they are meant to. It is the ability to wait without losing hope, to believe in the value of each moment, even when it feels slow or uncertain. Patience is not just about enduring time; it is about finding peace within it."

Eli closed his eyes, letting Cypress's words sink in. He thought about times when he had felt impatient, when waiting had felt like an obstacle rather than a part of the journey. He remembered wanting answers, wanting things to happen quickly, without delay. But Cypress's lesson was showing him a new way to see patience, as something active rather than passive, as a way of finding peace in the process instead of just focusing on the end.

"Patience also requires acceptance, Eli," Cypress continued, the voice soft yet firm. "It means embracing the present without constantly looking to the future. It is about understanding that everything has its season, that life unfolds at its own pace. When you practice patience, you allow life to happen as it is meant to, rather than trying to rush or control it."

Eli felt a sense of calm wash over him, as if Cypress's words were easing a tension he hadn't realized he was carrying. He thought about how often he had tried to rush things, how he had felt frustrated when things didn't go as planned. Cypress was showing him that patience wasn't about giving up or waiting aimlessly; it was about letting life flow, about trusting that everything had a time and place. It was a way of letting go, of allowing things to unfold naturally rather than forcing them to fit his expectations.

Cypress's voice was gentle as it continued, carrying a wisdom that felt timeless. "Patience also teaches you resilience, Eli. When you wait with an open heart, you grow stronger, learning to handle delays and disappointments with grace. Patience is the courage to stay present, to keep going even when things seem slow or challenging. It is a strength that builds over time, a foundation that helps you face whatever life brings."

Eli felt a deep respect for Cypress's words, a sense of awe at the idea that patience could be such a powerful force. He realized that patience was a kind of strength, a resilience that allowed him to face life's uncertainties without losing himself. It was a way of standing strong, of trusting in his own ability to handle whatever came his way. He understood now that patience wasn't just a passive waiting; it was an active trust, a belief that he could move through life without needing everything to happen all at once.

As he stood there, Cypress's branches swayed gently in the breeze, and Eli felt a sense of peace settle within him. Patience was teaching him to be present, to find joy in each moment, no matter how small. He understood now that patience was a way of seeing time as a friend rather than an enemy, a companion that helped him grow and learn in his own way.

Feeling inspired, Eli thanked Cypress, his heart filled with a quiet determination to practice patience in his life. He understood that patience wasn't always easy, but it was something he could carry with him, a strength he could draw upon whenever he needed it. As he left the grove, he felt as though he were walking more slowly, more thoughtfully, each step a reminder of the peace he had found within himself.

As he continued through the park, he noticed a small group of children playing nearby. They were trying to build a tower with blocks, but the tower kept toppling over, and one of the children was growing frustrated, his face scrunched up with impatience. Eli watched for a moment, remembering Cypress's lesson. He walked over to the children, kneeling down beside them with a gentle smile.

"Sometimes, things don't work right away," he said softly. "But if you take your time and try again, you'll find a way. Patience helps you see things clearly."

The children looked at him, their frustration easing as they listened. They tried again, this time taking their time, and slowly, carefully, the tower began to take shape. Eli felt a quiet joy watching them, a sense of satisfaction that came from sharing Cypress's lesson in a small, meaningful way. He realized that patience wasn't just something he could practice alone; it was something he could share, a way of helping others find peace and strength in their own lives.

Chapter 20: The Tree of Generosity

Eli awoke to a bright, sunny morning, his room filled with the warm glow of daylight. The lessons he had learned from the Wish Trees had begun to feel like a part of him, each one leaving a lasting imprint on his heart. They had shown him new ways to see the world, helping him to grow in kindness, patience, understanding, and strength. Today, he felt a lightness within him, as if he were on the verge of discovering something that would fill his heart with even more warmth. With a quiet eagerness, he got ready and headed toward the park.

The air was fresh as he made his way to the grove, the familiar trees standing tall and steadfast as they waited for him. He took in a deep breath, feeling a sense of gratitude for the wisdom they had shared, and allowed his eyes to wander, wondering which tree would guide him today. His gaze landed on a tree that seemed to radiate warmth and kindness, a tree with wide, welcoming branches and leaves that glistened in the sunlight. This tree had a gentle presence, as if it were inviting him with open arms, ready to share its lesson. Eli felt drawn to it, sensing that this tree had something powerful to teach.

He placed his hand on the bark, feeling a warmth spread from his fingertips, as if the tree itself were alive with kindness. A gentle, reassuring voice filled his mind, its tone soft yet full of strength.

"Hello, Eli," the voice said warmly. "I am Maple, the Tree of Generosity. My lesson is about giving from the heart, about sharing what you have with others to bring joy and light into the world. Generosity is a gift that fills both the giver and the receiver, creating a circle of kindness that grows with each act."

Eli felt a deep sense of peace wash over him, a feeling of connection to the lesson that Maple was offering. Generosity was a word he knew well, yet he sensed that Maple was teaching him something more profound, something that went beyond simply sharing things. It was about giving without expecting anything in return, a way of offering kindness that enriched both the giver and the one who received.

"Generosity," Maple continued, "is more than giving things; it is about giving of yourself, offering your time, your attention, your kindness to those around you. True generosity comes from the heart, a willingness to give simply because it brings joy to others. It is a way of spreading light, of making the world a little warmer, a little brighter."

Eli closed his eyes, letting Maple's words settle within him. He thought about times when he had shared with others, moments when he had given something he cared about to someone else. He remembered the joy that had come from these acts, a joy that seemed to fill him from the inside out. Maple was showing him that generosity was not just about material things; it was about giving a part of oneself, a kindness that reached beyond what could be seen or touched.

Maple's voice continued, soft yet filled with purpose. "Generosity also means giving without expecting anything in return, Eli. It is the choice to offer kindness without needing recognition or reward, to give simply because you have something to offer. True generosity is selfless, a way of connecting with others on a deeper level, showing them that they are valued and seen."

Eli felt a warmth bloom in his chest, a quiet happiness that came from knowing he could give without needing anything in return. He thought about moments when he had given something and waited for a thank you, moments when he had expected something in return. Maple was teaching him that true generosity wasn't about being noticed or praised; it was about the simple joy of sharing, a gift that brought its own kind of reward.

"Generosity is a way of creating connection," Maple said gently. "When you give freely, you open your heart to others, allowing them to feel a sense of belonging and warmth. It is a bridge between people, a way of bringing hearts together in kindness and trust. Generosity reminds us that we are all connected, each act of giving a reminder of the bonds we share."

Eli thought about Maple's words, feeling a deep appreciation for the power of generosity. He realized that each act of giving was a way of building connections, a way of creating a space where others could feel safe and valued. He thought about times when someone had given to him without expecting anything in return, moments when he had felt truly seen and appreciated. Maple's lesson was opening his eyes to the idea that generosity was a way of creating community, a way of showing others that they were an important part of his life.

"Generosity also brings joy to the giver, Eli," Maple continued. "When you give with an open heart, you fill yourself with a light that cannot be found in taking or keeping. It is a joy that grows with each act, a warmth that spreads through you as you share with others. Generosity is a source of happiness, a way of bringing fulfillment to your own heart while lifting others."

Eli felt a rush of happiness at Maple's words, a feeling that grew stronger as he thought about the joy of giving. He realized that each time he had given something to someone else, he had felt a special kind of joy, a happiness that was different from anything else. Maple was showing him that generosity wasn't about sacrifice; it was about a joy that grew with each act of kindness, a warmth that filled him as he shared what he had with others.

As he stood there, Maple's branches swayed gently, as if encouraging him to take this lesson to heart. Generosity was more than an action; it was a way of living, a way of offering kindness to the world with each moment. He understood now that generosity was something he could carry with him, a gift he could give every day, no matter how big or small.

Feeling inspired, Eli thanked Maple, his heart filled with a quiet resolve to practice generosity in his life. He understood now that generosity wasn't just about giving things away; it was about creating joy, spreading kindness, and building connections with those around him. As he left the grove, he felt a lightness in his step, a warmth that seemed to fill him from the inside out.

As he walked through the park, he noticed a young boy sitting alone, looking a bit lost and unsure. Eli felt a nudge from Maple's lesson, a reminder that generosity didn't have to be a big gesture. Sometimes, it was as simple as offering a smile, a kind word, a moment of connection.

Eli walked over, sitting down beside the boy with a friendly smile. "Hi," he said gently. "Would you like some company?"

The boy looked up, surprise flickering in his eyes, and nodded slowly. They began to talk, and Eli listened with his whole heart, offering his attention and kindness freely. He realized that even though he wasn't giving something tangible, his presence, his willingness to listen, was a form of generosity, a way of sharing himself with someone who needed a friend.

Chapter 21: The Tree of Humility

This day, each of the Wish Trees had shared a valuable piece of wisdom, helping him grow in ways he hadn't anticipated. Humility was a word he had heard often, but today, as he made his way toward the grove, he sensed that this lesson would reveal a deeper meaning, one that went beyond what he had ever thought humility meant.

When Eli arrived at the grove, he felt the familiar warmth surrounding him, the trees seeming to offer a quiet, encouraging presence. As he moved through the grove, he noticed a tree standing modestly on the edge, not particularly large or showy. Its bark was smooth and plain, with no distinctive markings, and its branches were not sprawling or grand. Yet, despite its unassuming appearance, there was a calm and steady energy about this tree, a feeling of quiet wisdom and strength. Eli felt drawn to it, sensing that it held a lesson he was ready to learn.

He placed his hand on the bark, feeling the cool, smooth texture beneath his fingers. A gentle, grounded voice filled his mind, soft yet filled with purpose.

"Hello, Eli," the voice said, its tone as calm and steady as a stream. "I am Alder, the Tree of Humility. I am here to teach you that humility is not about thinking less of yourself; it is about seeing yourself as a part of something greater, understanding that each of us plays a role in the world's story. Humility is the gift of perspective, a way to appreciate the beauty of others without diminishing your own."

Eli felt a flicker of recognition. Humility was a word he had heard many times, but he had always thought it meant downplaying himself, being quiet or reserved. Alder's words were opening his eyes to a different view, one where humility wasn't about making himself smaller but about seeing the world with a clear, balanced perspective.

"Humility," Alder continued, "is about knowing your strengths without needing to boast or compare. It is the choice to walk gently, to carry yourself with quiet confidence, respecting the gifts you have without feeling the need to outshine others. Humility reminds us that each person has their own gifts, their own unique light, and that we are all here to lift each other, not to compete."

Eli closed his eyes, letting Alder's words settle within him. He thought about times when he had felt the need to prove himself, to be noticed or praised. He realized that humility was about trusting in his own worth without needing to showcase it, a quiet strength that allowed him to be himself without comparison. Alder was teaching him that true humility wasn't about pretending to be less; it was about recognizing his own value without the need for recognition or validation.

"Humility also means being open to learning, Eli," Alder continued, sensing his thoughts. "It is the understanding that no matter how much you know or how skilled you are, there is always something more to learn. Humility keeps your heart open, allowing you to grow and evolve, to see each person as a teacher, each experience as a lesson."

Eli felt a warmth spread through him, a sense of peace that came from Alder's words. He thought about times when he had felt certain of his own knowledge, moments when he had closed himself off from others' perspectives because he believed he knew best. Alder's lesson was showing him that humility was a way of keeping his heart open, a reminder that there was always something more to learn, something he could gain by listening to others. It was a way of seeing each person, each experience, as a chance to grow, a way to stay curious and open to the world.

Alder's voice continued, calm and steady. "Humility also means being able to apologize, Eli. It is the strength to admit when you are wrong, to recognize your mistakes without letting them define you. True humility allows you to take responsibility for your actions, to seek forgiveness when needed, and to grow from each experience."

Eli thought about times when he had struggled to admit he was wrong, moments when pride had kept him from apologizing even when he knew he should. Alder's words reminded him that humility was a way of freeing himself from the need to always be right, a strength that allowed him to take responsibility without feeling ashamed. He understood now that humility was about growth, about learning from his mistakes and moving forward with an open heart.

"Humility also allows you to celebrate others, Eli," Alder said gently. "It is the choice to lift others up, to celebrate their successes without feeling diminished. When you practice humility, you see the beauty in others' achievements, knowing that their light does not make yours any less bright. Humility is a way to find joy in others' happiness, to be genuinely glad for their success."

Eli felt a deep respect for Alder's words, a recognition that humility was about finding joy in the success of others. He thought about times when he had felt envious or insecure, moments when he had compared himself to others and felt less than. Alder was showing him that humility was a way of celebrating others without feeling the need to compete, a choice to see others' accomplishments as a source of joy rather than comparison.

As he stood there, Alder's branches swayed gently, and Eli felt a sense of peace settle over him. Humility was teaching him to walk gently in the world, to see himself as part of a larger whole without needing to be the center of attention. He understood now that humility was a gift he could carry with him, a strength that allowed him to see himself and others with clarity and kindness.

Feeling inspired, Eli thanked Alder, his heart filled with a quiet resolve to practice humility in his life. He understood now that humility wasn't about being less; it was about seeing the value in everyone, including himself, without the need for comparison. As he left the grove, he felt a lightness in his step, a sense of peace that came from knowing he could walk through life with a gentle, grounded heart.

Chapter 22: The Tree of Courage

The morning sky was overcast, a deep gray with clouds that looked heavy with rain, and the air carried a chill that hinted at the approach of a storm. Despite the dreariness of the morning, Eli felt a sense of anticipation, an inner stirring that made him feel ready for whatever the day might bring. Each lesson he had learned from the Wish Trees had filled him with a unique strength, and today, he felt prepared to embrace something even more powerful.

After breakfast, he bundled up and made his way to the park. The wind whipped through the trees, making the branches sway and leaves dance, as though the grove itself were brimming with energy. As he stepped into the grove, he felt a wave of warmth wash over him, a familiar feeling that grounded him even amidst the swirling wind. His eyes scanned the trees, searching for the one that would guide him today. Near the center of the grove stood a tall, sturdy tree with branches that reached high into the sky, its trunk wide and weathered. This tree seemed to stand firmly against the elements, as if nothing could shake its steady, grounded presence. Eli knew instantly that this was the tree he had been drawn to.

He approached and placed his hand on the rough bark, feeling the strength of the tree beneath his fingers. A powerful, steady voice filled his mind, carrying a strength that felt unbreakable.

"Hello, Eli," the voice greeted him, deep and calm. "I am Oak, the Tree of Courage. I am here to teach you that courage is not the absence of fear; it is the strength to face fear, to move forward despite uncertainty. Courage is the ability to stand strong, to believe in yourself even when the path is unclear."

Eli felt a thrill of understanding, a recognition that seemed to settle deep within him. Courage was a word he had heard countless times, but he hadn't thought much about what it truly meant. Standing with Oak, he felt a new kind of strength, a reminder that courage wasn't about never being afraid. It was about choosing to act even when fear was present. Oak's words made him realize that courage was something he could carry within him, a quiet strength that would guide him whenever he felt uncertain.

"Courage," Oak continued, his voice steady and unwavering, "is about facing the unknown with an open heart. It is the willingness to take risks, to try new things, even if you don't know what will happen. Courage is not about being fearless; it is about trusting yourself enough to move forward, knowing that each step, each choice, brings growth."

Eli closed his eyes, letting Oak's words fill him with a sense of resolve. He thought about times when he had hesitated, moments when fear had held him back from trying something new or stepping outside of his comfort zone. Oak's lesson was showing him that courage wasn't about removing fear but about choosing to act in spite of it. It was a way of embracing life fully, of trusting himself enough to take risks, even when the outcome was uncertain.

Oak's voice continued, carrying a strength that seemed to fill the entire grove. "Courage also means standing up for what you believe in, Eli. It is the strength to speak your truth, even when others may disagree. Courage allows you to stay true to your values, to be authentic and honest, knowing that your voice matters."

Eli thought about moments when he had felt afraid to speak up, times when he had held back his thoughts or feelings because he feared judgment or rejection. He realized that courage wasn't just about facing external challenges; it was also about being true to himself, about having the strength to share his own beliefs and stand by them. Oak's lesson was teaching him that courage was a way of living with integrity, a choice to honor his own voice, even if it wasn't always easy.

The Oak's branches swayed gently, as if encouraging him to embrace this strength within himself. Courage was teaching him to walk his path with confidence, to face challenges with an open heart, and to believe in his own worth and strength. He understood now that courage wasn't just something he used in moments of danger or difficulty; it was a way of approaching life with a steady, grounded spirit.

Chapter 23: The Tree of Wisdom

It was a serene morning, the light filtering gently through his window. There was something different about this day, a sense of clarity that made the world feel calm and inviting. Each lesson he had learned from the Wish Trees had left a lasting imprint on him, and he carried these gifts with him as a quiet strength. Today, he felt ready for a new lesson, one that would help him understand not just himself but the world around him in a deeper way.

After breakfast, Eli made his way to the park, the familiar path through the grove welcoming him with its quiet beauty. The air was fresh, filled with the scent of earth and leaves, and each step felt purposeful, as though the grove itself were guiding him forward. As he walked, his eyes landed on a tall, graceful tree at the center of the grove. This tree had a presence that was both strong and gentle, its branches reaching high and wide, creating a canopy that seemed to embrace the whole grove. The bark was smooth and silver-gray, and its leaves rustled softly in the breeze. Eli felt a pull toward this tree, sensing that it held a lesson of profound importance.

He approached and placed his hand on the bark, feeling a steady warmth spread through him. A deep, wise voice filled his mind, carrying a calm that seemed to reach into his very soul.

"Hello, Eli," the voice greeted him, steady and kind. "I am Sequoia, the Tree of Wisdom. I am here to teach you that wisdom is more than knowledge; it is the understanding that grows from experience, from reflection, and from seeing beyond what is on the surface. Wisdom is a gift that deepens with time, a way of seeing life with clarity and compassion."

Eli felt a quiet sense of awe. Wisdom was a word he had often heard but had never truly understood. Standing with Sequoia, he realized that wisdom wasn't just about facts or ideas. It was something deeper, something that connected knowledge with understanding, a way of seeing life that embraced both the mind and the heart.

"Wisdom," Sequoia continued, "is about knowing when to act and when to wait, when to speak and when to listen. It is the balance between courage and caution, a way of living that honors both the seen and the unseen. True wisdom is a gentle strength, a light that guides without forcing, a truth that speaks softly but deeply."

Eli closed his eyes, letting Sequoia's words settle within him. He thought about times when he had acted quickly without fully understanding a situation, moments when he had been quick to judge or assume. He realized that wisdom was about more than knowing; it was about understanding, about listening deeply and responding with care. Sequoia's lesson was showing him that wisdom was a way of living with balance, a quiet strength that came from seeing life as a whole.

Sequoia's voice continued, calm and steady. "Wisdom also means being open to learning, Eli. It is the understanding that life is a journey of growth, that each experience, each person, holds a lesson. When you approach life with curiosity and humility, you open yourself to wisdom, allowing each moment to teach you something new."

Eli thought about times when he had been certain of his own knowledge, moments when he had closed himself off from new ideas because he thought he already knew the answer. Sequoia's words reminded him that wisdom was a way of keeping his heart and mind open, a choice to see each moment as an opportunity to learn and grow. He understood now that wisdom wasn't a destination; it was a path, a way of walking through life with a willingness to see beyond his own perspective.

"Wisdom is also the ability to see the interconnectedness of all things, Eli," Sequoia continued. "It is the understanding that each action has a ripple effect, that each choice touches others in ways we may not see. Wisdom reminds us that we are all connected, that our actions and words carry meaning beyond ourselves. When you live with wisdom, you live with a sense of responsibility, a kindness that considers others as part of your own journey."

Eli felt a deep respect for Sequoia's words, a recognition of the power of wisdom to bring people together. He thought about times when he had acted without considering how his choices might affect others, moments when he had focused only on his own needs. Sequoia was teaching him that wisdom was about seeing the bigger picture, about understanding that each choice was part of a larger story. It was a way of living with respect for the world around him, a reminder that his actions mattered, not just to himself but to everyone.

As he stood there, Sequoia's branches swayed gently in the breeze, and Eli felt a sense of peace settle over him. Wisdom was teaching him to live with awareness, to see each moment as part of a greater whole. He understood now that wisdom wasn't about being right; it was about seeing life with clarity and compassion, a way of connecting with the world that honored both his own path and the paths of others.

Eli thanked Sequoia, his heart filled with a quiet determination to live with wisdom. He understood now that wisdom wasn't something he could achieve or possess; it was something he could practice, a way of approaching life with a gentle strength and an open heart. As he left the grove, he felt a calmness in his steps, a sense of purpose that guided him forward.

The friend looked at him, surprise flickering in their eyes, and nodded slowly. They began to share something that had been on their mind, a worry they had kept hidden. Eli listened with his whole heart, offering no advice or judgment, only his understanding and care. He realized that wisdom wasn't always about giving answers; sometimes, it was simply about being there, offering a space for someone else to be heard.

Chapter 24: The Tree of Joy

Each lesson he had learned from the Wish Trees filled him with a quiet strength, a wisdom he could carry forward in all aspects of his life. Today, he felt a lightness in his heart, a sense that something special awaited him. As he made his way to the park, he walked with a feeling of anticipation, wondering what kind of gift the trees would offer him today.

The park was alive with sounds and colors, the breeze carrying laughter and the scent of blooming flowers. Everything felt vibrant, as though the world itself was brimming with energy. As Eli stepped into the grove, he felt the familiar warmth that seemed to welcome him with open arms. His gaze wandered over the trees, and his eyes landed on a tree standing near the edge of the grove. This tree was different from any he had seen before, with branches that stretched wide and high, almost as if they were reaching up to touch the sky. The leaves were a bright, shimmering green, each one catching the sunlight in a way that made the whole tree seem to glow.

Eli felt a pull toward this tree, sensing that it held something joyful, something he needed to experience with his whole heart. He approached and placed his hand on the bark, feeling a light warmth spread from his fingertips, as if the tree itself were filled with laughter and happiness. A bright, cheerful voice filled his mind, carrying a warmth that felt like a burst of sunshine.

"Hello, Eli," the voice greeted him, light and joyful. "I am Cherry Blossom, the Tree of Joy. I am here to show you that joy is not something you find; it is something you create. Joy is a way of seeing the world, a choice to find happiness in even the smallest of things. It is a gift you can give yourself every day."

Eli felt a thrill of excitement, a spark that seemed to spread through his whole body. Joy was a word he knew well, but Cherry Blossom's words made him realize that joy wasn't just a feeling; it was a way of being. It was a choice to look for happiness in each moment, to see the beauty in everything, even in the simplest of things. Standing with Cherry Blossom, he felt a surge of energy, a lightness that filled him with a sense of wonder.

"Joy," Cherry Blossom continued, her voice filled with warmth, "is a gift that grows when you share it. Just as the blossoms spread their beauty, joy spreads through each smile, each act of kindness, each moment of laughter. Joy is something you give to others simply by being present, by allowing yourself to feel happiness and share it freely."

Eli closed his eyes, letting Cherry Blossom's words fill him with a sense of peace and happiness. He thought about moments when he had felt true joy—times spent laughing with friends, the feeling of warm sunlight on his face, the sound of rain tapping against his window. He realized that joy was not something he had to chase; it was something he could create by simply appreciating the world around him, by being fully present in each moment. Cherry Blossom was showing him that joy wasn't about big events or grand moments; it was about finding happiness in the simple, everyday experiences.

Cherry Blossom's voice continued, light and filled with energy. "Joy is also a way to lift others, Eli. When you allow yourself to feel joy, you bring light to those around you. Your joy becomes a gift, a way to brighten the world for others, reminding them that happiness is always within reach. When you share your joy, you create a space where others feel safe to be happy, to let go of worry and simply enjoy the moment."

Eli thought about times when someone else's laughter or smile had brightened his day, moments when he had felt lifted just by being around someone who was joyful. He realized that joy was something he could share, a way of spreading happiness simply by being himself, by allowing others to see his genuine smile or hear his laughter. Cherry Blossom's lesson was opening his eyes to the idea that joy was not just a personal feeling; it was a gift he could give to the world, a light that spread with each act of kindness, each moment of happiness.

"Joy is not about avoiding sadness or difficulty," Cherry Blossom said gently, sensing his thoughts. "It is about finding light even in challenging times, about seeing the beauty in each moment, no matter how small. Joy is a strength, a choice to focus on what brings you happiness, even when life feels uncertain or difficult."

Eli felt a warmth spread through him, a quiet strength that came from Cherry Blossom's words. He thought about times when he had felt sad or uncertain, moments when joy had seemed distant. He realized that joy was not about ignoring these feelings but about finding ways to bring light into them. Cherry Blossom was teaching him that joy was a strength he could carry within him, a way to bring happiness into his life no matter what was happening around him.

Chapter 25: The Tree of Unity

Each tree had shared a unique lesson, weaving together wisdom, kindness, courage, and joy into a fabric of understanding that now felt like part of him. Today, he sensed that his journey with the Wish Trees would reach a profound moment, one that would bring all of these lessons together.

After breakfast, Eli walked to the park, feeling a peaceful sense of anticipation. The morning air was fresh and cool, and the park seemed especially beautiful, with sunlight casting a golden hue over everything. As he stepped into the grove, he felt a wave of warmth, the familiar embrace of the trees welcoming him. His eyes were drawn to a tree in the very center of the grove, one he hadn't noticed before. This tree was large and magnificent, its branches stretching wide, creating a canopy that seemed to shelter the entire grove. Its bark was textured and strong, and its leaves shimmered with a gentle light, as if they held a bit of the sun's glow within them.

Eli approached the tree with reverence, sensing that this tree held something special. Placing his hand on the bark, he felt a deep warmth, a connection that seemed to resonate in his heart. A voice filled his mind, strong and kind, a voice that carried both power and gentleness.

"Hello, Eli," the voice greeted him, steady and warm. "I am Cedar, the Tree of Unity. I am here to help you understand that we are all connected, each person, each tree, each part of life bound together in a web of harmony. Unity is the recognition that we are not separate but joined, each of us a vital part of the whole. It is the strength that comes from knowing that, together, we create something greater than ourselves."

Eli felt a shiver of understanding, a deep awareness settling over him. Unity was a word he had known, but he had never thought of it in this way. Cedar's words made him realize that unity wasn't just about being together; it was about embracing the interconnectedness of all things. Standing with Cedar, he felt a sense of peace, a feeling of belonging that seemed to expand outward, connecting him to everyone and everything.

"Unity," Cedar continued, his voice calm and wise, "is about seeing the beauty in diversity, understanding that each person, each being, has a role to play. Just as each tree in this grove has a unique lesson to share, each person has a light to bring to the world. Unity does not mean sameness; it means embracing our differences, celebrating them, and recognizing that they make us stronger."

Eli thought about Cedar's words, letting them resonate within him. He thought about his friends, his family, and even strangers he passed by every day. Each of them was different, each of them unique. Yet, together, they created a community, a world filled with diverse talents, perspectives, and experiences. Cedar was showing him that unity wasn't about erasing differences; it was about valuing them, understanding that they were what made the world rich and vibrant. He understood now that unity was a way of honoring each person's individual light, of seeing how these lights combined to create a beautiful whole.

Cedar's voice continued, soft and steady. "Unity is also about kindness, Eli. It is the choice to see ourselves in others, to extend compassion and understanding. When you approach others with kindness, you create a bridge between hearts, a connection that brings people together. Unity is built through love, through the willingness to see beyond ourselves and embrace the shared humanity that connects us all."

Eli felt a deep respect for Cedar's words, a recognition of the power of kindness to bring people together. He thought about times when he had seen kindness in action, moments when a simple gesture had brightened someone's day, creating a connection that transcended words. Cedar was teaching him that unity was built through acts of kindness, through the choice to see each person as part of himself. It was a reminder that every small act of love and understanding made the world a little closer, a little more united.

"Unity also means standing together in difficult times," Cedar continued, his voice filled with strength. "It is the courage to support each other, to lift each other up when the road is hard. Unity is not just about harmony in easy times; it is the strength to hold together through challenges, to be a source of strength for one another. When we stand together, we find a power that is greater than anything we could achieve alone."

Eli felt a warmth spread through him, a quiet strength that came from Cedar's words. He thought about times when he had faced challenges with his friends, moments when they had supported each other through difficulties. He realized that unity wasn't just about being together in joyful times; it was about standing by each other in moments of struggle, finding strength in one another. Cedar was showing him that unity was a bond that grew stronger through adversity, a connection that deepened when people came together to face life's challenges as one.

Cedar's branches swayed gently in the breeze, as if encouraging him to embrace this sense of unity within himself. He understood now that unity was not just a feeling; it was a way of living, a choice to see the world as a web of connections, each thread important, each person essential. He felt a deep sense of gratitude, a recognition that he was part of something much larger than himself.

Eli understood now that unity was not just about being with others; it was about connecting with them on a deeper level, seeing each person as part of his own journey. As he left the grove, he felt a lightness in his step, a warmth that made him feel connected to everyone he passed.

Don't miss out!

Visit the website below and you can sign up to receive emails whenever Finn Hayes publishes a new book. There's no charge and no obligation.

https://books2read.com/r/B-A-ADIVC-UBNIF

BOOKS 2 READ

Connecting independent readers to independent writers.

About the Publisher

Whimsy Tales Press is a creative powerhouse devoted to publishing exceptional children's books that spark joy, imagination, and lifelong learning. With a mission to inspire young minds, the company crafts stories that celebrate diversity, kindness, and the magic of discovery. Whimsy Tales Press collaborates with passionate authors and illustrators to bring captivating characters and enchanting worlds to life. From heartwarming bedtime tales to empowering adventures, every book is designed to entertain while fostering empathy and curiosity. Committed to excellence and inclusivity, Whimsy Tales Press ensures that each story leaves a lasting impression, encouraging children to dream big and believe in endless possibilities.

Milton Keynes UK
Ingram Content Group UK Ltd.
UKHW020914291124
451807UK00013B/919